BIG JOHN

Florence Elizabeth McClinchey
(1888 - 1946)
is also the author of
Joe Pete
Re-published by Ziibi Press, 2018
First published by Henry Holt in 1929

BIG JOHN

Florence Elizabeth McClinchey

Edited by Phil Bellfy

ZIIBI PRESS
SAULT SAINTE MARIE, MICHIGAN
2018

© 2018 by Ziibi Press, Philip C. Bellfy, PhD, Editor.

ALL RIGHTS RESERVED. This book contains material protected under International and Federal Copyright Laws and Treaties. Any unauthorized reprint or use of this material is prohibited. No part of this book may be reproduced or transmitted in any form or by any means, electronic or mechanical, including photocopying, recording, or by any information storage and retrieval system, except for the use of brief quotations in a book review, without express written permission from Ziibi Press.

Published in the United States by Ziibi Press.

ISBN- 978-0-9830894-1-4

First Printing: May, 2018
Second Printing: July, 2018

Ziibi Press
Phil Bellfy, Editor
5759 S. Ridge Rd.
Sault Ste. Marie, MI 49783
<ZiibiPress.com>

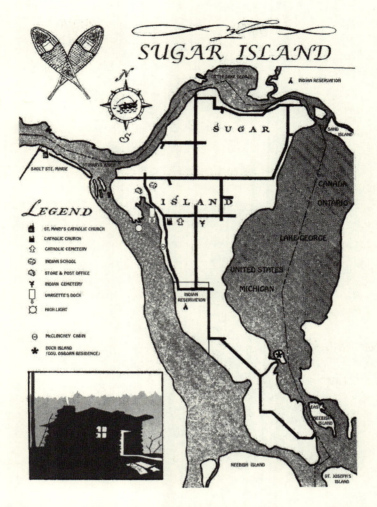

This image has been adapted by the Editor from a map drawn for the Hamilton family as a guide to the location of their cabin on Sugar Island, circa 1930. Their cabin was near that of Governor Osborn. Historians have indicated that there were several schools, churches, cemeteries, stores, docks, and post offices on the Island during this period. The Editor has placed those structures on the map approximately where they are mention-ed in the novel.

The image in the lower left of the map was adapted by the Editor from the dust jacket image, by Carrol Snell, that appeared on the hardcover edition of McClinchey's novel, *Joe Pete*.

INTRODUCTORY NOTE

Florence E. McClinchey was born in Sault St. Marie, Michigan, of English and Irish parentage, and has lived there most of her life.

After graduating from high school, she went to normal school at Ypsilanti. She taught in the Sault until her parents died, after which she attended the University of Michigan, where she earned a Master of Arts degree.

From the university, she went to Mount Pleasant, where she taught in the English Department of the Central State Teachers College during the summer, and, as late into the year as is possible, lived on Sugar Island, the setting for both of her novels, *Joe Pete*, and *Big John*. She calls her log cabin on the island her home, and says the friends she made there will always be her best friends.

"My friends tell me that I am hard to get acquainted with and that I am too reserved," wrote McClinchey. "But I believe it was these two qualities which enabled me to become friends with the Indians and learn much of their legends and tales. I belong in the woods, and feel more natural there than in any other place. I am an expert in a canoe, and know how to manage a launch in a heavy sea. Those two accomplishments are the ones about which I always boast."

"Florence McClinchey is, indeed, exactly the right person to study those Indians who still preserve their tribal identity, to live near them in a neighborly way and, unobtrusively, discover their way of thinking, discover how they feel about the whites who have shunted them off to reservations, here and there," writes Oakley Johnson. "And she has had exactly the right opportunities to do so. Born in upper Michigan, she was able from the first to observe the Ojibway across the conventional distance that separates them from white society; and, later, she lived for many summers on Sugar Island, the locale of her story. As she says of the Indians, 'one never knows the Indians familiarly for they are too reserved. But they have come to know me and have told me much of their old tales and legends. These were what I really was after until I realized that their lives were better stories than any they were telling me.' From this environment, and with this material, she came to the University of Michigan, --came, as she says, because she 'wanted to find out the best way' to tell the story."

The result of her labor is *Joe Pete,* a first novel of undisputed excellence. Florence McClinchey has unearthed a world that has never before been exposed to public gaze, a world distant yet near, filled with poignancy, rooted in the very bed of America, and she has drawn it with a freshness and a richness that augurs well for the newer American literature.

Adapted by the Editor from the December 1929 Book League Monthly "Christmas Edition" of *Joe Pete*.

Florence McClinchey, was critically injured in an automobile accident on May 26, 1946, in Mt. Pleasant, Michigan. At the time, she was Associate Professor of English at Central Michigan College (now Central Michigan University). She died of her injuries on June 13.

P.C.B.

A NOTE TO READERS ON LANGUAGE

There are no gender-specific pronouns in the Ojibwe language. The reader should be aware that the author uses *he* and *she* interchangeably to indicate that the characters are speaking in their native tongue.

PREFACE

My journey with *Big John* and my Aunt Florence McClinchey has been a very long one. It started one summer when I visited my mother, Mary Wilcox McClinchey, in the Sault. When it came time to leave, she gave me the manuscript of this book, and told me to take it with me. After all, my Aunt Florence --my father Norman McClinchey's only sister-- had written it! I took the manuscript home with me, put it in a box on the top shelf of my bedroom closet, and promptly forgot it.

Twenty-eight years later, my Mom got a phone call from a man named Bernie Arbic, who was researching my Aunt in connection with the novel *Joe Pete* that she had published in 1929. He was intending to discuss her work in a book of his own that he was writing about Sugar Island, which is the setting of *Joe Pete*. My Mom invited him over to her house on Riverside Drive. The view out of her front window looked straight across the river, appropriately, at Sugar Island.

I was a very small child when I knew Aunt Florence, and my memory of her is vague. She would come to my parent's house during the summer to visit. At Christmas, she would send me books. I only wish that I had been older, and more able to appreciate who she was.

Sue (McClinchey) Anderson

EDITOR'S NOTE

What follows is the edited manuscript as it was given to me (which included the cover design). It was copied into PDF format; OCR was then used to edit the text which was then compared to the manuscript for accuracy. I have made no changes to the manuscript (retaining the author's spelling, paragraph breaks, etc.) except to correct obvious typographical errors. Megwetch (thanks) to the many people who read and commented on the manuscript, and to those who helped me locate the errors. I apologize for any errors that may have been overlooked.

P.C.B.

To Professor and Mrs. E.A.Walter
and Marie and Eric Walter.
Ann Arbor, Michigan

The characters in *Big John* are entirely fictitious, and any resemblance to persons living or dead is coincidental.

ACKNOWLEDGMENTS

The suggestion for the book-jacket and the drawing of the Ojibway symbols are the work of Frances Gibson Fitch, of the art department of Central Michigan College of Education. The colors used are the primary ones known to the Indians of this region.

The Ojibway symbols used are authentic. Some were taken from School-craft's _Indian Tribes_, some were collected and given to the author by Father William Gagnieur, S.J., and a few were collected by the author.

"I faint and falter under Thy chastening rod.
My burden is too heavy. Tomorrow I die."
Anonymous

SYMBOLS USED FOR CHAPTERS

I - Spirit -- symbol of a man whose totem is the snake.
II - The Child -- symbol of mystical power
III - The Indian School -- symbol of instruction in knowledge and magic
IV - Big John goes to Wish -- symbol of the moon, flaming and propitious
V - Waubegoon -- symbol of a man walking at night
VI - White-Tipped Arrow -- symbol of magic skill with arrow
VII - Winter of Change -- symbol of an encampment
VIII - Waubegoon Pays the Forfeit -- symbol of power over the heart of a woman.
IX - Madeline -- symbol representative of womanhood
X - Celestina -- symbol of sociability
XI - Jennie – a flag, used to decorate a grave
XII - The Foreigner -- a flag, used to mark a grave
XIII - Kahnee -- symbol of the domestic circle, or a homemaker
XIV - Kababishe -- the screech owl, symbol of evil or misfortune
XV - The Last Omen -- symbol of death
XVI - Big John -- symbol of the death of a man whose totem is the eagle
XVII - Afterglow -- symbol of time passed

CHAPTER I
SPIRIT

**SYMBOL OF A MAN WHOSE
TOTEM IS THE SNAKE**

SPIRIT

Big John sat on the lowest step of his front stoop and pondered deeply. As he rubbed his fingers through his black hair, standing it more on end than usual, he was entirely unaware of his surroundings. Before him the blue lake stretched out fifteen miles straight ahead, until it was lost in a far, green horizon of August heat-haze. Gulls soared and planed and dipped over his head, and called raucously to each other as they flew. Down at the dock Young John tinkered at the launch engine, which had not been working smoothly for a long time. When he dropped a wrench suddenly, the sound smote sharply against the cabin and returned the echo to him, seemingly doubled in volume. Occasionally he glanced toward the house and his father, but he kept on working. A maple tree in the front yard had one branch of scarlet flaming against its green, and Young John wondered idly for the hundredth time what had made that branch turn color when there had been no frost and no other leaf in the woods had changed. But always he returned to his work.

From the living room which opened from the step, came sounds of industry as Mrs. Big John and her oldest and youngest daughters, Kahnee and Waubegoon, talked softly and musically while they wove their fine, velvet-smooth splints and sweet grass into beautiful baskets to sell to the remaining hay-fever tourists. They glanced often toward the window, where Jim, the eldest, sat laughing at the comic strips in an old newspaper. They could hear Jennie, the second daughter, singing to herself a crooning little Indian song about the owl that flew in the night, as she sat on the steps behind the house and watched interestedly while Abe Shingoos fashioned grotesque figures from the pile of common red clay, which he dug from their hill and kept close at hand always, under some wet canvas. She wondered about his long, slender fingers as they cleverly and swiftly patted into shape an odd form or caricature of someone they knew, and she also scanned his face intently for some resemblance to Joe Pete, his half-brother, whom she loved deeply. Ever since Abe had come to live with them, when Joe Pete went away to school, she had watched Abe to find some traits the brothers might have in common, but she had found none. Suddenly, with a flourish typical of him, Abe finished the image he was making and with his own impish grin held it up for her inspection and approval. They both burst into quick laughter, for the little figure was exactly like Mr. Vargatte, the storekeeper for whom Abe worked, and yet was not at all like him if they examined each feature separately. However, the general resemblance was so apt that anyone would have recognized, immediately, Mr. Vargatte smiling over the counter at a customer. Abe carried the clay around to the front of the cabin to show Big John, but seeing him sitting there absolutely oblivious to all movement and sounds around him, again walked back to Jennie and shook his head. Neither Abe nor Jennie could under-stand something that seemed to be worrying the family today.

In the mind of Big John there was being fought a battle between the old superstitions and religion of his people and the new faiths the Indians had been taught by the whites. This struggle had been with him for a long time, and yet he was undecided, so he overlaid the new on the old ideas until he could come to some final conclusion. In his thinking he was like a naive, yet shrewd, child. And now in this quiet daylight, he almost wondered if this thing they had seen the night before had actually happened. Over and over again the whole experience went through his mind, and he thought that of all the queer things which had occurred in his life, that was the queerest. His thoughts went far back, even to the events of his youth. There was that time he had attempted to guide two white men to the lost ledge of gold and the spirits to whom the gold belonged had made his wits hopelessly muddled and he could not find it, though he knew as well where it lay as he did where the old maple stood in his front yard. Could he believe this thing which had happened last night was a sign which his forefathers would have understood, and should he and Young John search for the cause or report to the storekeeper first! Again he pondered over what had happened to them.

They had stopped at the Settlement on their way home from town the night previous. They had bought some groceries at the store and had visited for an hour or more with Mr. and Mrs. Vargatte, who had had a letter from Joe Pete saying he would write soon to Big John and tell him some important news. Their discussion of the letter and its import was leisurely and long, as usual. When they finally pushed their skiff out from the store dock, the August moon rose full and round and red from behind the trees, and they could see with marvelous distinctness every small stick and floating object on the water. They had yet six miles to row, but the Indian fashion of rowing is efficient and takes little effort; they had the swift current with them; and Big John knew every rock and sand bar as intimately as the city dweller knows the bumps and cracks in the cement walk in his block. The high range lights and red and white channel lights meant to Big John what street signs mean to the town man. They talked amiably for a time about the big passenger boat which had been off-schedule to town; the good clothes which Mrs. Big John had taken in exchange for her 'baskets; the new boat which Frank Mokuk, their neighbor was building for a tourist; the location of a huge white birch, the bark of which they needed for new cossos; and then lapsed into their customary pleasant silence. Big John filled and lighted his pipe without once interrupting his deft manipulation of the steering paddle, then he passed the tobacco over to his wife. She had forgotten her pipe, but she filled her mouth with the fine-cut tobacco and began to chew with slow enjoyment. Jim refused when it was passed to him. They were happy. It was good not to be living in a town! Only the water dripping from the oars as they lifted for the next stroke, the occasional creaking on the oarlocks, and their casual remarks about the passing, brightly-lighted freighters revealed their presence on the river. There was a law that small boats must carry lights after sundown, though this rule was seldom obeyed. A lantern was in the boat, but they never had time to fill it with kerosene. They could always tell a searching Coast Guard Patrol that the light had only just gone out. One by one their landmarks went by; the lone Shingwauk Point with the hidden, ugly reef beyond; a white, flashing channel light; the Frechette Rock; the wide sand bar over which their boat could pass easily; the low range light. The high range light shone to their right now. The Big Johns were always glad to see this light, with the smaller, yellower light from Green-Cloud's cabin shining on the shore behind it, for at the end of one short half hour after they passed this cabin they would be home. As they neared the High Light they watched the shore closely to see if the lamp would be burning in Green-Cloud's cabin. His place was behind the Light and partly hidden by it, and Green-Cloud had bitterly resented the "Government" placing it there, where it blocked his view of the lake and the freighters which passed close to the Island shore at the point. Green-Cloud wanted a clear horizon! But he was very old now, probably one hundred, and active resentment was a thing he had not felt for a long time. His shoulders were mightily stooped as though he had carried an over-loaded pack for many years up a steep hill. All day he sat in the sun, smoking and mumbling to himself, as old, old men of all tribes will do until there comes an end to time. No one knew what his thoughts were, for the thoughts of aged persons go traveling far back into the old tangled folk-trails, where it is hard for others to follow them. Now that he was too feeble to move about, he was again bothered by the bars of the High Light across his vision, and discontent had settled on his face. The Big Johns knew he had not been so well as usual, and for that reason they watched for his light as they followed the shoreline more closely than was their custom.

As they swung around High Light they saw Green-Cloud's small, white-washed cabin standing out clearly in the moonlight, almost startlingly separated from the thick woods so close behind it. There was no sound now but the licking of the freighter-ripples against the shore. And as they came nearer they saw there was no light in the cabin and the door was partly open. There must be something seriously wrong if Green-Cloud left his door ajar, for when darkness came he closed all doors and windows tightly to keep out the wicked Manitous, such as the will-of-the-wisp, which could creep through the tiniest crack in a wall and steal a man's spirit, or send it wandering over unknown trails while he lay asleep. They looked questioningly at each other and in their black eyes was a great fear as they asked softly if they should stop now to investigate or wait until morning. The door of the cabin creaked slightly and they stopped rowing, to listen in the silence. Then the door seemed to move, as though Something, groping about in that dark interior, had just happened to touch the door, and through the familiar feel of it had known again that it was the way out of the cabin. The Big Johns were bewildered. They could see nothing, but they were somehow unable to shift their hypnotized eyes from that door which opened into blackness. As they watched, the door swung gently but inevitably back all way on its hinges, as if a Thing, soft but very heavy were pushing it open into a cave of darkness. They waited, fascinated. And then that Something took shape out of the black night of the cabin's interior, a horrible shape. A large, flat head appeared a few inches above the doorsill, then came slowly out, trailing behind it a huge slimey body. It lay just outside, sluggishly, its enormous scales and lidless eyes gleaming in the silver moonlight. "Aih-ah," softly groaned Big John in terror, breaking that spell which held them there against their will, shivering, "It is the totem of old Green-Cloud!"

As though the faint sound of his voice had disturbed it, the Snake raised its head and started slowly toward the water and they now realized the great size of it. Its eyes were phosphorescently gleaming, and as it crawled languidly down toward them, like some awkward, gigantic Thing which did not yet know the use of its new body, it left behind it a deep slimy groove, dug into the soft ground by the weight of its body. It slid into the lake with a thick, greasy splash, and ripples widened out to their skiff where they sat helplessly, waiting. With the noise of that splash the men came to their senses and rowed as they never had rowed before. The boat shot through the water with a loud, gurgling at its bow as they sped down the lake toward their own dock, still a long way distant.

Seemingly without the exertion of movement the Snake overtook them. As it came closer and stared at them, it occurred to Big John, even in his terror, that there was something human and very wistful in its eyes. It swam beside them, quite close, as though wanting companionship on some strange journey it must undertake alone. It was supernaturally repulsive and awesome, yet it made no attempt to attack them. Finally, from sheer fright-weariness, they gave up the attempt to keep ahead of it. Like a monster from one of their own tribal tales, it kept close to their boat, staring at them, until they reached their own pier. It ceased following them then and lay so still that its length could hardly be seen on the black water, but its lifted, weaving head with the glittering eyes watched them until they reached their own door. Then it raised itself in the water, looked at them strangely once again, and turned like a flash of blurred Northern Light. Where it swirled, there rose into the air a small fountain of gushing water from its swiftness, and it headed back up the lake in the direction of Lake Superior, where float eternally the happy islands of the Indian dead. For an instant or two the moonlight picked out and sharply outlined every scale on the rapidly turning body, then it merged gradually with the dim horizon and disappeared from their sight. Without stopping to watch the course it took, the Big Johns rushed into their cabin and closed the doors and windows, and not until then did they feel secure. For hours, quietly so as not to disturb the sleeping younger folks, they talked of the Snake, but could only conclude that it was one of the "old" signs that Green-Cloud was dead, and in the morning Big John must go over to that cabin and see what had happened there.

Now, Big John realized, it was the morning, and he, superstitious as any member of his tribe and dreading the job ahead of him, sat on his sunlit stoop, wondering if the folk-magic which vouchsafed such signs to the Ojibways would ever entirely disappear from them as it had from the white races, and if they could ever completely lose faith in their earlier beliefs. Now the time had come to prove to himself, past all future doubt, the truth of the sign. With a feeling of awe he contemplated the thing he intended to do.

A sputter of the engine and then a steady purr told him it was in working order again. He called to Young John, and Young John, who was still watching his father closely, sensed the call and shut off the engine, the better to hear. Big John told him to fill the tank with gasoline and went to the house to get his hat and to call Jim. Mrs. Big John looked up from her weaving and there was a question in her eyes. He nodded in answer and went out of the house. Jim followed. As they walked down to the boat Abe Shingoos came tagging along at their heels and looked so wishfully at the launch that they took him with them. One never knew when Abe might be useful, for he was keen witted and there was a hardness about him which made him unafraid of anything. As they puttered again with the engine they told him something of what had happened and what they expected to find. He looked curious, but only nodded and said nothing. He could occasionally talk to Jennie, whom he liked better than anyone else because she understood him and expected nothing from him, but to the others he seldom betrayed any of his thoughts or feelings.

When they landed in Green-Cloud's little cove they could see a furrow in the ground, leading from the cabin and down to the lake. Big John rubbed his head, tipping his hat askew. Then it was not a dream they had had! Dreams do not leave behind them tangible evidence! They saw the door pushed back as far as the hinges would swing. Together they entered, leaving the door wide open to let in all the light possible. And there on the floor, with content showing plainly on his face, lay old Green-Cloud. His expression was serene and Big John thought he seemed to have been freed from that secret irritation. Maybe now he could see as far as he wished and without looking through the iron cross-bars of the High Light. They did not need to touch him to know he was dead. They gently picked him up from the floor and placed him on his cot in one corner of the room. After they had covered him with a piece of quilt, Big John spoke. "Then it was a sign from old and it told us Green-Cloud was dead and on his trail to the Place of the Dead. He was even then stepping over the End's Edge, when we saw his totem."

Jim shrugged his shoulders, but Young John, as always, answered his father. "It is all strange yet in my head. I have not your wisdom and I have not had time to think through it, so I do not know what to answer."

They closed the cabin door against prowling small animals and went on up to the store to report the death to Mr. Vargatte, who would in turn report to the proper authorities. They did not tell him of the sign and its meaning for them and that they had known of the death in that way. Big John said merely they had gone to visit old Green-Cloud and had found him dead on the floor, and Mr. Vargatte, knowing his Indian friend well, did not question him, though he sensed there was something more than had been explained by Big John. They did not talk much about it, for they had discovered from past experience that even the best and most understanding white people, such as Vargatte truly was, do not believe in Indian or any other kind of magic.

Big John trusted the Vargattes enough to ask them to come while they buried Green-Cloud in the hidden Indian place where their dead had been buried for many ages on a mound which was so ancient that none of the present generation of Indians had any idea of its origin. So, just two days later, Mr. and Mrs. Vargatte stood at the top of the mound, so old that huge trees grew from its summit, watching while strong men carried old Green-Cloud toward them up the steep slant, climbing the steps cut into the clay sides of the mound. As they listened to the Indian women singing, Mrs. Vargatte trembled and clung tightly to her husband's arm, which he quite instinctively put about her in a protective gesture. For they were two solitary white people, suddenly stepped back into old folkways and impending dangers of an alien race, and in the Indian voices, though they were singing familiar Christian hymns, translated into their own language, there was the sound of wolves howling and the rhythmic beating of ancient medicine drums. These people the Vargattes had believed they knew intimately and liked well, seemed aloof strangers inhabiting a place peculiarly their own, who did not need or want a condescending friendship from any other intruding race.

Mrs. Vargatte was relieved when it was over and she walked with Theophile away from the lonely mound and down the sunny trails back through the woods to the store and reality again. There was an elusive beauty about the secret place which somehow made her feel dejected.

When they reached the main trail she became animated and happy again, so much so that her husband realized she was feeling a cessation of some strain which he did not experience. He looked down at her as she walked beside him, and was puzzled at her supersensitivity to the feelings and thoughts of others and her deep insight and toleration of the foibles of average folks. Long ago she had told him that when she felt an unusual or deep emotion, or knew her friends were undergoing trials, she always heard from a distance deep, mystic pipe-organ tones. She had tried through every common-sense theory to explain to herself the origin of these sounds and thus rid herself of them, but finally, because she loved the ethereal beauty of them, she had liked to believe that she was actually listening to some great melody of human existence.

Big John also went quietly and gladly home, and walked all that day about his common duties in a dream, because of an immense satisfaction which had come to stay with him forever, and his new, firmer belief in the ancient magic and power of his tribe.

CHAPTER II
THE CHILD

SYMBOL OF MYSTICAL POWER

THE CHILD

Big John's Red-Cow was lost. That in itself was not so unusual, for this obstreperous old Red-Cow had one peculiar idiosyncrasy she loved, above all other things, to wander alone through the woods and along the shore. This time was different from all other times, however, for she had not deigned to come back home again, and had now been gone three days. Mrs. Big John insisted that unless some person were milking her daily, she would be "spoiled" and of no use to them when she did condescend to return. The day was warm and sunny and the clouds were sailing huge and white in a sky of deep blue. The light breeze was cool from miles of water-crossing. Big John was so stirred by the beauty of the day, after a week of rain, that he suddenly decided the old Red-Cow had been gone long enough, so he called the favorite son, Young John, the tall, slim. fifteen-year-old lad, and the boy came to him with glad, silent speed. He was always delighted when his father invited him to do anything, or go anywhere with him. Big John told him they were off to hunt for Red-Cow, so Young John called to the dogs and they took the trail which led down along the edge of the Woods and followed the shore-line. Old Red-Cow had a fondness for wet sea-weed, washed up on the beach by the Fall storms.

They followed her tracks where she had wandered along the sandy beach, and laughed to themselves as they read the trail-marks and saw her dainty avoidance of the wettest spots along the way she had chosen. They liked old Red-Cow, in spite of her bad habit of wandering away, and her queer little lady-like manners afforded them a constant source of amusement. They were glad of an excuse to be in the woods on such a perfect day and they followed the trail steadily and carefully, though without any obvious searching for tracks, even where the trail was beaten hard on the drier ridges. The half-wild dogs ranged far ahead, sometimes at each side, and their shrill barking resounded through the quiet woods. Ahead of the dogs birds flew in all directions and red-squirrels chattered shrilly and jerked their tails up and down in their safe perches on high twigs as the dogs stood underneath and yelped excitedly at them. To the men everything seemed carefree and happy in the September woods and they were constantly amused at the tricks of the smaller woods-animals, as they walked quietly along after the dogs.

They had gone probably three miles from the cabin, and were wondering just how far old Red-Cow had strayed this time when they were startled by a change in the note of the barking of the dogs. They stopped and listened, puzzled. Then, simultaneously, they hastened as fast as they could along the trail toward the dogs. They knew the mongrels had found something which was strange to them; their sharp, ecstatic yelps told the Indians something very unusual had been discovered. So they hurried, for once shaken out of their serenity.

As they came around a bend in the shoreline they found themselves in a natural, shallow cove, where the smooth beach sand ran far out into the water and formed a perfect breakwater, so not a ripple disturbed the silence of the place. The noise of the dogs was so menacing that not a bird sang, not one small animal moved. Here it seemed to the men that even the woods had taken on a change in character in this protected spot. Big John thought swiftly that he had never seen the leaves so motionless, the trees so still. The men stood bewildered for a moment, then noticed that the dogs were standing and snarling at something which was hidden from them behind a huge boulder close to the shore, where the sand met the woods. The hair stood out on the dogs' necks like the bristles of porcupines, and their teeth were bared, white and threatening, yet they were obviously afraid to attack whatever was behind the great stone.

Big John and the boy hesitated a few moments, while devil-tales of their ancestors flashed through their minds. But the sun was shining brightly! In all the old tales moonlight was the time for magic! Big John laughed silently and shook his broad shoulders as though ridding them of a weight of superstition. Young John watched his father and became more daring. They crept toward the boulder, and as the men approached, the dogs regained their confidence and renewed their staccato yelps. Big John ordered them to him, Young John enforced his father's commands with a switch, and the dogs were driven reluctantly away from the stone. They squatted on their haunches, watching the men, waiting with muscles all tensed to spring, and occasionally licking their lips. They were a vicious, haphazard breed, and were wickedly ready to attack anything which was helpless and at their mercy. The men were surprised that they had not already attacked.

In his moccasins Big John crept up to the stone and nothing could have heard his approach. Behind him, armed with the switch he had used on the dogs, came Young John, also noiseless as the quiet woods. Yet nothing stirred, except the deep-green reflections in the water of the pine trees as they swayed in a faint breath of wind high up in their tops. Big John went around one side of the boulder and at the same time the boy crept around to the other side, to trap whatever was hiding there so closely. Then they stopped as though they had been halted by a hand pulling them backward, and gazed at each other as if they were wondering whether they were seeing the same thing. With their bellies hugging the sand the dogs crawled closer to the men and watched avidly to see what their masters would do with this strange quarry. Big John removed his hat and scratched his head as he always did when he was stumped by some uncommon occurrence.

"By God!" he said in English, for it is impossible to swear in the Ojibway language, "This is one damn queer thing that has happen!"

Behind the enormous stone lay a white woman, stretched full length on the sand, and beside her, lying between her body and her outflung arm, was a tiny baby, fast asleep. The woman looked as if she were sleeping too. but the men knew she was not, nor was she feigning sleep. No woman, no matter how courageous she might have been, could have lain there so unconcerned and motionless, or kept on sleeping, through the noise the dogs had made such a short time before. Most women screamed when one of the dogs came near them. The men did not touch her immediately. They looked guardedly at each other and asked in the Ojibway, which she would not likely understand if she did hear, where she might have come from. Neither could suggest an answer to their own questions. The baby was quite evidently not more than two weeks old.

Then the men began to search along the shore. They would see yet in the moist sand at the waterline the marks where a blunt-nosed boat had been pulled quite high on the beach while someone had carried this human flotsam from it and hidden her in the shade behind the boulder, where she could not be seen from a passing rowboat or canoe. Someone had also broken a branch from a pine close by, and had smoothed away all betraying footprints. The woman might have lain there for weeks without being discovered if they had not come hunting old Red-Cow, for that shore was lonely and deserted, and there was no house in a stretch of many miles except their own. They scanned the cove, and cut through the woods across the point to the next one, where they looked out over the water as far as they could see for signs of the small craft which had landed the woman such a short time before that it seemed impossible it could have gone from sight. Out in the lake, big red freighters ploughed the water into rims of white at their bows as they carefully picked their way up through the channel and on to the big locks. The enormous size of them, and the tiny specks upon them which were men, only emphasized the seclusion and secrecy of the shore upon which the Indians stood. These boats represented a life from which the woman had been dropped upon them here, a life entirely out of the scope of the imagination of these two Islanders.

After surveying the lake for a long time, hoping to get some clue, they shook their heads and walked slowly back across the point to where the woman still lay motionless beside the stone, the dogs watching her closely. The sun had crept around and now her body was lying half in the bright light which glared down upon the hot sand. The baby woke as they again came near and began to rub its eyes aimlessly and whimper a little. The dogs went back into the woods and began again their chase of woods things. Then the men set to work. There was only one thing they could do. They dared not leave the woman here, and there was no place to take her but to their own home. At first they did not know if she were dead or not, but when Young John bent low over her he heard her slow breathing and was glad she was alive.

They made a stretcher of their shirts slipped over two poles, and were very careful that nothing might slip and let their burden drop to the ground. Outside of directions from Big John they did not talk, for this was the most serious thing which had ever happened to them, and they had no words to express what they felt. Neither did they know what to do, for this was beyond their woods-knowledge; they were uncertain just what the results of this episode might be; and they were more than a little afraid of the white man's law if the authorities should have to be called in. It was lucky, they thought, that Mrs. Big John was home, and was not only skilled in the Indian medicines but had learned some things about nursing from the French women in the Settlement, for whom she had worked.

When the litter was finished they placed it on the sand close to the woman. Then they hesitated and again looked at each other, Big John just as questioningly as Young John. Theirs was, in a manner, a foolish reaction to the situation, but never before had they touched a white woman, except to shake hands with Mrs. Vargatte. But they had to do it. Carefully as any woman might, they lifted their unmoving burden upon the stretcher and cautiously placed the baby beside her. Then they each took one end of the poles and began their laborious homeward journey. She was a heavy woman, solidly built and large boned, and they had to rest frequently. The old Red-Cow was entirely forgotten and abandoned to her wandering. The baby cried as they jolted along, but the woman never moved or spoke. They began to fear she was dead, or might die before they reached their cabin.

Mrs. Big John saw them coming, and waddled to open the door for them, but without removing the pipe from her lips. Queer things had been carried many times to her house to be nursed back to health and strength, and she had long ago ceased to be surprised at anything Big John did to ease one in pain or trouble. Their home had been always open to stray children, and to men and women long forgotten by their own people, and now why should it not open again for a white woman who needed help! This was as natural as anything else in the life of the woods, for what was dropped as worthless by anyone on the trail of life might be salvaged by the next traveler if he found it useful. When she saw the double load they carried she grunted her sympathy, and commanded them to place the woman on the bed in the big living room downstairs. It was the cleanest room on the Island, and the bed-clothing was as fresh and white as washing could make it. The men placed the woman and baby upon the bed and then left the affair to the women. Big John went out to the beach and sat upon an upturned rowboat, and scratched his head as he asked himself where this woman had come from and how exactly had she gotten here. Young John raced as fast as he could to the cabin of Mindemoya, usually called the Very Oldest Mother, who, though very aged, was skilled in the use of powerful herbs. He was to ask her to come to their cabin to help in this situation. If the Very Oldest Mother was not there he was to wait until she returned or search until he found her, for she was a famed wanderer. She was seldom in her own cabin, for her knowledge of medicines and her gift of story-telling made her a welcome guest in even the most crowded Indian cabins, where she was urged to abide as long as she chose. She had become almost a legendary figure to the Indians, for not even the oldest could remember when she was not already an old woman.

While she waited for the boy to return, Mrs. Big John ran her fingers gently over the baby's fuzzy head, after, she had removed the cloth which had been wrapped about it, and exclaimed with delight and admiration. At this unaccustomed sound, Waubegoon came running into the room and gazed at the baby, and then curiously at the woman in the bed. "Is it to be ours then, Mother?" she asked, giggling. "May we keep it, do you suppose, like those other small ones we have had? It is long since we have had a child in this cabin, and they are fun."

"I hope we may keep this one," answered Mrs. Big John solemnly. "But look at this baby, little Giggler! Do you not see she is a Manitou baby and he may not allow us to have her? Look at the red-gold of her hair, and how it already curls around my finger, and I believe she is not yet more than two weeks in age. Such hair is the sign the Manitou touch, and if we could own her she would be a fetish to the tribe. Her hair is soft like the silken threads of the young birch, curling in the wind," she continued musingly. "Queer it is that none of our children has such hair; that it appears only among the whites."

Her mother's unwonted garrulity excited Waubegoon. She had been told of the old belief that a red-haired person is blessed or "touched" by Manitou. She held out her arms coaxingly and her mother placed the baby in them and then turned her attention to the woman. Waubegoon's mouth dimpled into smile as she quieted the child and watched her mother undress the woman and work tenderly over her. Nothing had happened for a long time. Waubegoon was glad of this excitement. Maybe the woman would go away again and leave this small thing with them. Such things had often occurred on the Island and the woman certainly did not seem to care much about the baby. She would not even awaken and look at it.

Just then Big John ushered the Very Oldest Mother into the room. After the women had greeted each other he asked in a whisper, "Do you know what is the trouble with the lady? Is she going to waken?" Jane Big John nodded. "In the Settlement, once, the white doctor gave Madame Delongue some strong medicine after she broke her arm, which made her sleep a heavy sleep just as this one is doing. Someone has given her too much of that same strong medicine and it probably will be a long time until she wakes. Then she will be very nauseated. You can smell the stuff she has taken. Her eyes may be open tomorrow."

The Very Oldest Mother grunted corroboration to that and added for Big John's benefit, "It has been known in Indian medicine ever since the beginning of knowing, that we can use certain herbs in our own woods to produce a similar sleep. We keep that wisdom hidden, that wicked persons may not use it for secret evil purposes. Only a few of us are allowed that knowledge."

Big John was relieved and went out to get the work finished, and after he had gone both the Indian women tried to make the strange woman comfortable.

But Mrs. Big John and the Very Oldest Mother were mistaken. The sleep upon this woman was more powerful and not the same as that the white doctor had induced in Mrs. Delongue. True, she half-aroused and drank some milk two or three times, but it was more than a week before this Strange Woman --for so they called her who had come to the Island so mysteriously from some hazy horizon-- regained consciousness. When she did finally come to life from her heavy daze, she looked about her and her face became drawn and livid with a desperate fear at the sight of all the alien leaf-brown faces around her. They politely said nothing, waiting for her to speak first. She could not talk with them because she obviously could not speak or even understand the broken English which they used when they must, the French which they spoke fluently, or the Ojibway, which to her was only a jumble of meaningless musical sounds. She spoke in a language they had never heard and they looked upon her in even greater wonderment. She must have come from a very distant country indeed! What could they do about it! In vain they now questioned her almost frantically in the three languages at their command, for she did not comprehend a word they spoke. Finally she groaned despairingly and turned her face to the wall. They knew she was terribly afraid, and tried by gestures to console and reassure her, but she refused to answer or turn to look at them. As she seemed too weak to leave her bed, they gave up their attempts to interrogate her further, and left her to a slow recovery.

Later that week Mr. Vargatte came with Abe, at Big John's request, to see the Strange Woman. Theophile looked down at her with sympathy plainly showing in his face. At first the Woman drew away from him, but after watching him for a while as he sat with Big John, she appeared to feel confidence in him and tried again in her foreign language to talk with him. He also could not understand her, and though he shook his head to indicate that fact to her, he patted her on the shoulder and she did not shrink from his touch.

"She has had some very dreadful shock, that woman," he told Big John, "and we may never discover where she did come from. I have read about people who have been hurt or badly scared, and they forget their names and everything that has happened to them. Some have been found in places far from their own, and gradually came back to full remembrance. Let her rest here where she is until she becomes strong again. By that time Telesphore Dinet, that smart half-breed cousin of mine, will be returned from his travels, and it may be that he can understand and speak with her when he comes to visit us. You remember how he talks many strange languages and it is not so long to wait when we can do nothing anyway."

Telesphore Dinet! It was a name to conjure with among the Indians. His influence was great as that of Big John himself, yet there was deep friendship between them and no jealousy. True it was that he was a half-breed, but one in whom were combined the best traits of both races, and he was more shrewd and clever than most white men. He was an interpreter for the immigration department when he was not wandering in foreign countries, and he knew the customs of all the races of whites and could speak in any language, just as Mr. Vargatte had said. So it was all left gladly until Telesphore should return. By this time, too, they had become accustomed to the presence of the Strange Woman and the Child in their cabin, and did not want to lose them. After a time the Woman also became used to the friendly dark faces peering at her at all hours of the day, for Indians from various parts of the Island, who had heard of her and the baby, came to see what kind of person she might be, and to wonder about her, and to admire the red-gold of the child's hair. It seemed that each day the hair became redder, with glints of deeper gold, and they became more convinced that Manitou had sent her to them as a good-luck sign.

When the versatile Telesphore arrived, two weeks earlier than they all expected, he came immediately to Big John's cabin to see the strange woman. Telesphore had an insatiable curiosity. All the Big Johns gathered around them with as much eagerness as Indians ever betray, anxiously and almost fearfully waiting to see if he could talk with her and discover her history.

The Woman lay and gazed stupidly through half-opened eyes at Telesphore, as if in self-defense, and seemed entirely uninterested, as though she had settled into a lethargy of hopelessness. Telesphore spoke to her in several languages, trying them rapidly one after the other, a few words of each, but with no response. He looked dolefully at Big John, for his linguistic ability was his one very great talent and he hated to fail in front of them all. Finally he stooped closer and examined her features minutely for a few moments; his eyes excitedly glistened and he turned to Big John. "I think she is a Swede, her," he said, "and I believe I can talk enough of that to question her."

Then he tried another kind of speech, which to the listening Indians seemed strangely guttural at times, and then smoothly-flowing. Her eyes widened and sharply came awake all at once, and she answered him. From the tone of the voices they knew he was questioning in a language with which he was less familiar than the others he spoke, and she was trying hard to answer and asking some of him. He was coaxing in his dramatically tender voice and her face was tight and her voice husky with the effort she was making to remember. It seemed a long time to the Indians that Telesphore conversed with the woman, and then almost reluctantly turned to Big John to report the meager result. She was Swedish, he believed, because she spoke that language, though some Nordic people spoke two or three, but she could not tell him where she had lived. She could remember nothing about her people or her husband --if she had one. She did not know how old her baby was, or its name or her own. She did not know how she happened to be in their house. Beyond the moment she had awakened from her long sleep in their cabin, her mind could not force itself to go, and before that awakening she could not remember anything which had happened to her, or any people she had known. She did not know she had been brought to the Island in a boat until Telesphore told her, and then she had answered that she had never seen such a boat. What seemed to Telesphore more deplorable than the lack of knowledge of her past was that she did not know where to go or what she was going to do to earn her living. Her bewilderment was pitiful, translated precisely by the temperamental Telesphore.

"Tell her, Telesphore," said Big John in Indian, after he had listened, apparently unmoved, to what the woman had said, "she is not to do any more worrying about what she will do. We will do her thinking for her. We will find a place for her here on our Island and take care of her. Say that she must stop this uneasiness, for Mr. Vargatte says it will prevent her from getting her memory back again. We like her and the red-haired baby, and no trouble will come to them while they are with the Ojibways."

Telesphore gladly translated, and the woman seemed more contented than she had been since coming to them. But Big John, though he had spoken confidently, did not know just what he could do about her situation. Would Indians be allowed to keep this white woman who had been so strangely thrust upon them? What would white man's law say about her? There were many phases of this predicament which he must discuss with Mr. Vargatte, now that they knew something about the woman, and the sooner it was discussed and decided, the better everything would be for all of them.

Just before they left the cabin to talk out on the stoop, Telesphore had an idea and went again into the room where the Woman was. She looked at him gratefully and talked rapidly to him. The Very Oldest Mother sat by the bed and stared at them as Telesphore answered the woman and then proposed something to her. For a long time she looked at the baby cuddled in the Very Oldest Woman's arms, almost as if she believed the child did not belong to her, and then nodded. He laughed merrily and hurried out to the kitchen where Big John was waiting.

"Big John," he said, with an infectious laughter running along in his words, "none of you thought to name the red-haired baby. She is probably now one month of age, and she must begin to be called by a name. The thought came to me that she is as beautiful as my sister, though indeed my sister has not the red head, and I wished her to have the same name. I have already asked the Strange Woman, and she agreed it was well to follow our custom of naming a child, and so the baby will carry the name of my sister. It is a most respectable name for any child, and beautiful as well."

"Which sister?" asked Big John dazedly, for the idea of any other name than the Child had never entered his head, and he could not think as rapidly as Telesphore.

"My most charming sister," answered Telesphore, solemnly enough now. "Deneece, the sister who sings in the church with the voice of the angels! Deneece shall be her name and it may bring luck to the child. Who shall say!"

Big John nodded, much satisfied that this name had been proposed for the baby. Then Telesphore added, almost bashfully, "You should know, Big John, the Swedes are grand race of big men and women, very honest and clean too. If this baby and woman have been abandoned by her husband, then he is a bad member of a decent race; just as we have bad Indians mixed with the good ones. All races have evil men among them and they must not be judged by that. I have traveled more than most men, and this is a big truth I tell you, my friend."

Big John smiled at this warm-hearted Telesphore. "That is great truth," he agreed, "but we all wish to believe our own is the best race of peoples."

When Telesphore left the cabin, singing happily and loudly, the Strange Woman sat up in her bed and smiled at the Very Oldest Mother who was holding the baby close in her withered arm. A strange iciness in the Woman seemed to have been broken by Telesphore. The Very Oldest Mother looked at her understandingly, and immediately the two women knew a bond of affection had formed between them, despite the difference in age and race.

After the store had closed that night, Big John knocked and then entered the Vargatte living room. There he and Mr. and Mrs. Vargatte talked until late in the night, discussing the problem of the Strange Woman frankly and in all its phases, and what could or could not be done with her. There were institutions, Mr. Vargatte told Big John, that the white people supported, where similar such stray folk were kept. He thought that in such a place she would probably be well cared for and would have good food. He could not believe, however, that she would be happier or better in an institution than where she was.

Finally they decided that for the present, as soon as the Woman was strong again and not so timid, they would install her in Green-Cloud's empty cabin, after cleaning it thoroughly. Then they would all contribute for a time to her care, until she might be able to fend for herself, though they doubted if she would be capable of this until her memory returned. They could teach her to weave and sell her baskets with their own. She might even find a job in the Settlement later. The cabin was close enough to Big John's so they could watch over her until she could work, and possibly, in a home of her own she would accept responsibility and thus come easier to a remembrance of her past life. The cabin was furnished enough for comfort, and Mr. Vargatte and Big John would assume full obligation for her support. Others would be willing to help for a time, and to provide food and wood and other necessities.

Big John went striding out of the store with a broad smile on his face. Now they were sure, because of Mr. Vargatte's help and influence, of the red-haired baby for a time anyhow, and the luck which was sure to accompany her would more than compensate for any trouble they might have in obtaining food and comforts for her. Food was the greatest problem, for the shelter of Green-Cloud's cabin was adequate and the beach was covered with driftwood; enough to last a hundred families for a lifetime. Baskets could be traded for enough suitable clothing, for the townswomen were usually generous in their bartering for Indian baskets. He took off his hat and joyfully rubbed his thick hair all endwise.

"By God," he exclaimed in fervent though broken English, that feller Vargatte, she's ---she's---" Then he grinned and reverted to his favorite words of encomium as he said low, only to himself, "She's damn fine feller! I like her good, me!"

CHAPTER III
THE INDIAN SCHOOL

**SYMBOL OF INSTRUCTION IN
KNOWLEDGE AND MAGIC**

THE INDIAN SCHOOL

The lake was massed with white-capped seas whipped high by a November wind which all night had howled down from the north, over the Canadian hills. The Island, looming enormous against a black, cloudy sky, had lost all its October color and seemed even more isolated and solitary than usual. Big John beat his way skillfully through huge waves which threatened to swamp his launch, and made a masterly landing on the lee side and in the shelter of the big cribs which supported the store dock. Then he shook off the little pools of icy water which had splashed over the mail sacks, threw them, still dripping, over his wide shoulders and started down the board walk to the store. He was so accustomed to the admiring stare of people that he was entirely unconscious of it, and also of the fact that he himself, even in modern clothes, was a representation of the ideal Indian figure which an artist would have given much to use as a model. At the store he handed the sacks over to Mr. Vargatte, who had seen him coming and was holding the door open for him against the wind, and seated himself upon a covered nail-keg near the wall, waiting to see if there might be a letter for him. He had had a rough trip down from town with the mail and his face was stinging from the buffeting of the wind. The late Fall days were shortening rapidly. The store was dimly lighted by one kerosene lamp, and it swung in the draft when the door was opened occasionally, creating queer, gigantic shadows which moved back and forth across the floor and walls. A small, yellow kitten came from behind a meal-sack and rubbed against Big John's boots. As Big John waited he drowsily watched Theophile Vargatte sorting the letters, and the movements of his hands, as he placed the mail in the various boxes were so quiet and smooth that Big John was soothed almost to sound sleeping as he sat. His eyes gradually closed. He began to think of spring-new leaves moving silkily in a soft dawn breeze, but at that moment the last piece of mail was dropped in place, the leaves disappeared from before his eyes , and he was awake.

"Two for you, Big John," called Mr. Vargatte, and Big John smiled at him sleepily. So he sat on until all the others in the store had bought their groceries and had gotten their mail. It was closing time. Last moment buyers hurried through their purchasing to be home in time for supper, and as they opened the door and passed out, Big John saw that the night had come, black and stormy. Mr. Vargatte locked the door and turned to his friend. Then Big John rose from his nail-keg, almost reluctantly, stretched himself, took his two letters and followed Theophile into the living room which opened directly from the store. They pulled their chairs close to the big coal-stove, then Big John handed the letters to his friend.

"Maybe you read him then and tell me what he speaks?" he questioned.

Theophile nodded. "One is from Jeanne and the other is from your Joe Pete. I notice that Delima has also received a letter from Jeanne. Something must be up in the wind between those two sisters."

Big John smiled but did not answer. The mystery of postmarks and the wonder of the written word which conveyed speech would always be things of white man's magic to him even though he carried these missives over his shoulders jauntily. When magic was concerned one did not hurry, so he was content to wait. The room was quiet while the Frenchman read both letters and then re-read them, almost as though he had forgotten Big John's presence. The Indian did not seem uneasy. He listened to the wind tearing around the store building and the tapping of an elm branch against a window, but from under his eyelids he was intently watching every changing expression of Theophile's mobile face, and also reading. When the other man looked up, Big John appeared again to be half-asleep, but Theophile was not fooled.

"This is most serious, Big John, my friend," he said solemnly, "and all plans for our Joe Pete may yet have to be altered."

"Read to me those things they speak on the paper," said Big John, also in French, "and after we will talk of him."

"Which letter will you hear-first?" Vargatte asked.

"The one of our Joe Pete," replied Big John, and even in front of the eyes of the white man he could not keep a certain joy out of his face. His love for the boy was sincere and his faith in him was limitless. What if things were serious, as Mr. Vargatte said!

They had faced serious things before, and in any crisis that occurred he knew Joe Pete would not fail him.

Mr. Vargatte grinned rather mirthlessly and began to read. Knowing the temptations the boy would meet in the outside world, Mr. Vargatte could not have the boundless faith the Indian had. The wind blew harder, in furious blasts, like an accompaniment, Theophile thought moodily as he turned the pages of the letter.

Big John, my good friend.

I write to tell you bad news which nobody can help. The men Jerry works for are sending him far to the west, where there is yet much timber, Jerry says. He did not expect this to happen when he asked me to live with him and go to school. He must go or lose his job. He can't afford this. He says he will be gone maybe fifteen or twenty years, he says, for it will take so long to cut those big trees. He does not like to go for he wants me to go to school, but that can't be now. When Jerry must be gone for this long time Jeanne must go too. If you and Mr. Vargatte think it is right I will go to the Indian school for it is our own school. Jerry says it is better I go in this state and not to a school far away. He does not want me to go alone far away from you. Here it will cost no money and Indians from all places come here. If you do not like this I will come home. Jerry wants Mr. Vargatte to write very soon what you want us to do, for he is worried. Jeanne is writing to you and to Madame Vargatte.

I am your good friend   Joe Pete.

As Mr. Vargatte read the letter, Big John's eyes assumed a defensively detached look, for he was more disturbed than he wanted anyone to know, even his friend. His concern was for the boy. Joe Pete would miss Jerry and Jeanne more than they would understand from anything he would say to them. For Joe Pete had already learned that people of his race smiled and went on, even when their hearts were breaking over losses and injustice, and this is what he must do. They had not wanted him to go to an Indian school, for they had, more than anything else, desired that he should learn the customs and the exact speech of the whites. This letter showed he had done well in his learning of it. They had heard many stories of the terrible treatment Indian children received in the Indian schools; such stories of abuse and rotten food that Big John was startled and dismayed at the suggestion that Jerry thought Joe Pete should go to such an institution. None of the Island children had gone to an Indian school, so they had no first-hand knowledge of conditions as they actually were, but even white people did much loud talking in criticism of the abuse of helpless Indian youngsters who were so unfortunate as to have to attend any state school for Indians.

 Yet Joe Pete must not return to the Island. He must accomplish the job he had been sent to do. He had borne bitter poverty and neglect, and there might perchance be more of both to be endured on his Trail of Life. He must be fitted to meet any situation which might arise in which the Indians would need a champion. Hazily Big John realized that even with Jerry smoothing the way there were many temptations in city life which Joe Pete had never met on the Island, where life is lived simply and without many complications. The tales of Indian schools might be untrue. Such stories may have gone uncontradicted by those in authority because they felt they were too unreasonable to be credited by sensible people. Maybe, if the white men who had charge of the school were wise and farseeing, they might teach the boy the things he needed to know, even better than teachers in the public schools. From close contact with the Indian they should have a clearer understanding of the Indian problems and might suggest a solution to all their troubles" He had met many splendid white men. In fact, his best friend was Mr. Vargatte, a white man as, loyal as any Indian. And there was Jerry - there was Jeanne-- --their own priest-- --and-----

 He was brought back from his cogitations by Mr. Vargatte's voice saying gently, "Let's not do any thinking or worrying about this question which is so close to our hearts until I read to you what Jeanne says about it. We know she has a wise head, trained by study and thinking, and it is possible that she has worked out a way which may settle these difficulties for us. She has written very clearly and now hear what she says."

My dear Monsieur Big John,

This will be a long letter, but you will have to be patient with it for there is much to say. If you have read Joe Pete's letter first --as I am sure you have—[Big John and Mr. Vargatte grinned at each other.--she knew them so well] you will know something of the situation we are facing. Jerry has just had this offer to go to Tacoma and feels that he must take it, for it means probably twenty years of work with a good salary. We could take Joe Pete with us, and that is what Jerry would like to do, but that is not the place where he is to work out his problems and he is working for those very definite things which you want him to learn before he returns to the Island. In spite of drawbacks he is doing well

Because we have concluded that it is unwise to take him with us, we feel that he should be in a school where he will get individual help and attention. He is finding life here in the city a problem and much different from what it was on the Island. There he had things hard, but he was free from certain temptations found here in this "big city" which are many and hard for the boy to resist.

He should have a year or two right now of intimate help and understanding advice, such as Jerry would have given him, until he has become adjusted to things and has developed a new set of values. For that reason Jerry went to the Indian school down here and investigated it thoroughly. He realized how prejudiced most people are, because of the stories about these schools; and, to make sure, he questioned the children there as well as the teachers. He came home perfectly satisfied to have Joe Pete go there for a year or two, for the teachers are nice and the superintendent, Mr. Brand is one of the finest men you could meet. Jerry told him exactly what the Island situation is, and Joe Pete will get special consideration in his work. He is genuine and sincere and interested in the boy. We are sure Joe Pete will be comfortable and happy, for all the children Jerry questioned seemed contented and fairly happy there.

Mr. Brand told us that Joe Pete can stay there only for the next year or so, because he has practically finished the academic work which they cover in this school. But he can learn a great deal from association with other Indian boys of his own age, and from the teachers, and he can learn about the farm and trade end of the work. About that I have written in detail to Delima, and she will explain it all to you. He cannot enter without your permission, so we want you to have Theophile write and tell us soon what you decide to do.

Since he is already here his transportation will cost nothing, for Jerry can drive him over before we leave and get him settled. He may come home for summer vacations if he pleases, but we would suggest that he remain there until he completes the work and then go on to a higher Indian school to finish his high school education. By that time he will have become adjusted to city life and things will be easier for him. Jerry has had all his prejudices against Indian schools wiped out completely by talking with Mr. Brand. The school is a short way outside a small city, probably a mile, and Jerry says there is a pleasant woods on the grounds. It all sounds so favorable that we are much happier about the whole thing than we thought we could be. We are going to miss him terribly. Mr. Brand is planning a trip to the Island next summer and he is going to talk with you, Big John, about many things.

The beautiful basket Madame Big John sent us is admired by all our friends. Thank her again for it.

Our remembrances to all the family.
       Sincerely.,
         Jeanne.

Just as Mr. Vargatte finished reading the letters, Delima and Armand came into the room and told them both to come to supper. There at the table, snugly set in the kitchen, they four discussed the problem from all angles, supplemented now by the information of the work done in the Indian school, which Jeanne had told Delima in her letter. Painstakingly Mrs. Vargatte explained classes, reports, trade-work, "credits," and the thousand things of schoolwork Big John had never heard of before. But always they returned to the original question of whether Joe Pete would learn in this school, and later in the higher one, what would be of most benefit to the young Indians on the Island. Delima told the men what Joe Pete's schedule would be for the day, every minute from six in the morning until nine at night, according to the plan which Jeanne had sent her, and not one of the activities which the superintendent had listed as part of the day's work and recreation seemed unwise or useless to any of them. Jeanne had also said in her letter to Delima that Mr. Brand would write them any further information or answer any question about the school and its work that they might wish to ask. It was plain to be seen that Jerry liked and trusted this superintendent, and they were satisfied to depend on Jerry's quick, keen judgment of men. The fact that he was so positive this was the right thing to do was what finally decided Big John "and Theophile to give their consent.

The important question was at last settled and the letter was written. Both men drew a long breath, and Mrs. Vargatte laughed at them. "We can surely trust our Jeanne and Jerry to know what is best for Joe Pete," she said. "And this next month our own Armand goes to St. Josephs, where he shall study to become a priest. It has been lonesome for him here since Joe Pete went, and we have decided that he may go. Now both our boys will be away and we shall so miss them. Joe Pete will in time return to us, perhaps, but Armand will stay out in that so-big world--" Her eyes glazed with tears but her smile remained.

Big John was still so immersed in thought that he did not notice Delima or comprehend her announcement about Armand, but Theophile and the boy looked at her sensitive, animated face and soft brown eyes, and were once again deeply thankful that the flu had not taken her from them. She was so beautiful; so irresistibly loving and gentle! There was no other woman like her. After a time Big John sensed the silence of the others and caught their expression as they looked at Delima. He smiled, as only Big John could, and said quietly, "You are good 'oman, Madame Vargatte. Ver' good." She shook her head and laughed.

"He is right, my mother," Armand said, too seriously, Delima thought. "Monsieur Big John has given you a splendid compliment. And if I can possibly become as kind and noble a priest as is Father Lalliere. I shall also be giving you a splendid compliment."

"You are gallant, my Armand," approved his father. They were all thinking of the old priest who had lived many years among his beloved Indians. Wherever his Indians went, there was his parish. Through the years he had followed them, by canoe, dog-team, sailboat, or on foot, no matter what the weather might be, and his experiences were numerous and uncommon. In his battered suitcase was his altar. Wherever he set up his altar, there was his church, in boat or shack or wilderness. Looking at his thin, ascetic face, one thought of pictured saints, and almost expected to see a sudden halo about his head. Armand aimed high to approach the unworldly devotion and humility of this scholarly priest, loved by everyone, even those not of his faith. They sighed and then smiled at the boy, slim and tall now as he had grown older, and he knew he had their complete approval of his decision at last.

Big John left the store, still thinking deeply. He was rather lost in this maze of white man's ideas, because he could not think rapidly as they did. But he could trust these honest Vargattes. They had already done much for him, and he knew they stood with him, ready to do more. It was brought home to him even more forcibly the truth of Telesphore's words that in all races there are many honorable men. He would have many things to explain to Mrs. Big John and she would probably clear up any remaining doubts about the wisdom of what they had decided to do with her probing, pointed questions. He left his boat at the store dock and started homeward on the old, well-beaten trail.

As he walked sturdily along he realized that the wind had died and the young moon had come from behind the great bank of clouds which had darkened the day. Heavy woods-odors came to his sensitive nostrils. Twigs cracked under his heavy boots. The moon's silver was suddenly poured over all the old familiar landmarks. He saw the dim trail leading up to his cabin and heard the glistening leaves of the old oak which he had always known, whispering even now after the wind had apparently died. His dock stretched far out into the moonlit water, and for a moment he wished his launch were tied there instead of at the store dock. For a few moments he stood motionless, simply looking at these things which made life for him, suddenly realizing his deep appreciation of them all. In his own inarticulate fashion he loved and felt beauty as keenly as an artist. What was Joe Pete thinking tonight, so far from it all! The boy loved these things too. Rather wistfully Big John shook his shaggy head at the thought, rubbed what seemed to be a mist from in front of his eyes, held his head high and stepped heavily up on the stoop to let Mrs. Big John know he was home again. He seldom was so late. Yet he knew that when he opened the cabin door he would find her waiting, confident and unquestioning. There was no other woman who could quite compare with Mrs. Big John! Then he remembered the way Theophile had looked at Delima. Quickly his nostalgic mood changed. He laughed, spontaneously, joyously. Not even that fine person, Madame Delima Vargatte, wife of Monsieur Theophile Vargatte, was any finer than his wife, an Indian, but Madame Jane Big John. He opened the door with a snap and hurried into the yellow-lighted room.

CHAPTER IV
BIG JOHN GOES TO WISH

**SYMBOL OF THE MOON,
FLAMING AND PROPITIOUS**

BIG JOHN GOES TO WISH

Another long northern winter had passed and May had come with its usual rush of flowers and leaves. Big John for once was glad the winter was over. He wondered, as he walked down the old trail to the store, if he were growing old. He did not know exactly what his age was, but he figured that he must be past sixty. Carrying mail through the blizzards and deep drifts of many winters had been no easy task, though he still held his perfect record of always getting the mail delivered on time. He was not accustomed to mental uneasiness, and during the worst of the cold weather when they were shut away from the rest of the world, there had been many things to worry about. The foreign baby was so young that her magic had not grown powerful enough to help. Bad moonshine whisky had crazed many of the young fellows and there had been quarrels and savage fighting among them, which Big John had difficulty in straightening out again, despite his tact and authority. Mrs. Big John had not been well. Her knees were swollen and almost useless. There had been times when Abe Shingoos seemed to forget all his newly-acquired, decent habits, and had reverted to the little devil he had used to be. Even Jennie could do nothing with him. Kahnee wanted to marry Moses Katemishkid, --the Sluggard, they called him because of his shiftlessness-- and even though they liked Moses, the marriage would mean one more for the family to support. Waubegoon, only sixteen and the youngest of his girls, had become entranced with a jaunty, yellow-headed Irishman who had taken up a forty-acre homestead down on the lower end of the Island, near the place where the new boat channel was to be dredged by the "Government." "Outlanders" they called all those who were not natives of the Island, and held aloof from them, not because of dislike, but for lack of interest or curiosity. Big John did not want any of his children to marry whites, and this alien fellow had an ugly old mother of evil temper, who would perforce live with a new wife because she had no other place to go. Waubegoon was too young to realize the unhappiness resulting from such a situation, even among people of one race. Jennie and Young John had done their utmost to keep up the morale of the household, but now that Spring was here, Jennie had unexplainedly developed a frantic discontent with things as they were on the Island, and wanted desperately to go to the Indian school where Joe Pete was; to learn other things than basket weaving. She had argued doggedly that Joe Pete would have so much more learning than she, he would look upon her with contempt when he returned. To satisfy her, Big John had to consent to her going in September. At the end of the month Young John would be leaving to work down-river on the dredge, and his immediate departure seemed to be the culmination of Big John's troubles. Jim wanted to go to Canada to work in the lumber camps. Soon he and Mrs. Big John would be alone. After being accustomed to a houseful of young people this would be hard! He walked on listlessly, and deep within him was a queer nausea of loneliness, which was such an unusual feeling that he was scared. At heart Big John was a Child, with a child's firm unreasoning belief in magic and sorcery. All his contacts with white people, and even with their religions, had not eradicated any of it. He wished fervently that he could carry in his pocket a talisman as powerful as the one carried by the medicine man, John Shahwinigan, The thought flashed through his mind that some enemy might be wishing "bad medicine" on him. But, despite his yearning for ease from this fretting which was almost painful, he felt better as he tramped through the woods.

Beauty always soothed Big John, and this day was a perfect one. The late afternoon sunlight filtered through the tree branches down across the trail in great splashes, yet was checkered with the faint shadows of young leaves. Wooly-napped, tight-fisted ferns were pushing up through the leaf mould. Irregular patches of snow still lay under the thick pines and balsams, and the dropped needles of these trees formed daintily traced green patterns on the white of the snow mounds. Shining brown pools were held back by the rivulet-worn roots of trees, mirroring blue sky and white sailing clouds. And there came to his ears, through all the glamour and fragrance of the Spring woods, a regular boom, boom, boom, like the beating of time-mellowed drums. The sound cheered him, for it meant to him that the Indian women were following the old customs, and were out in the forest getting their ash timber for baskets. Memories came back to him of trailing along behind his mother when she went after the ash. Almost involuntarily he turned from the beaten trail and made his way toward the place where the women were working. As he came closer he heard the ageless song, chanted by many generations of Indian women as they cut their "timber."

> "Sharp is the axe.
> It bites deep and clean
> Into the ash tree.
> The sap runs from the wound,
> As blood from a stroke
> A warrior bears;
> Bears bravely,
> Without moan or sound.
> The slim tree falls,
> Our bright axe is ----------"

The song broke as they saw him coming, then when they recognized him they continued it.

> "The slim tree falls
> Our bright axe is keen.
> Our labor is now
> But just beginning.
> The women work always,
> Weaving strong baskets,
> Weaving beautiful baskets,
> With strips of clean ash,
> With white strips of ash.

A small group of women were working slowly and very deliberately. Waubegoon and Jennie were felling one tree, their axes striking regularly in turn in the same spot. White chips, glistening and sticky with sap, flew from beneath their shining blades. Waubegoon in childish fashion had braided a garland of pink "spring beauties" and yellow adder's tongues, everywhere under-foot, and had hung it about her neck. It swung to the rhythm of her movements. When he came toward them they smiled at him, but kept on working. Kahnee and some older women pounded with the blunt end of the axe blade on the trees already felled, and each time they

41

struck, that measured booming echoed through the woods and seemed the pulse of the song. The old women laughed as they separated the loosened strips of pounded ash from the hard core of the tree, coiling and placing the strips in brightly colored baskets. The Very Oldest Woman sat upon a small piece of folded tarpaulin with her back against the sun-warmed trunk of a tree, watching them with her keen black eyes while she smoked a worn pipe. A mongrel cur lay close to her, asleep, with his head on a bit of her skirt. Every little while his legs twitched as if he were dreaming of running. In one of the still pools two small, silent children sailed boats made from scraps of fallen bark. The leisurely scene was familiar to Big John, yet it thrilled him as it stirred old memories.

Much to Big John's astonishment and annoyance, two other men came down the trail and stopped to watch the women as they worked. Like an owl, Moses Katemishkid peered about short-sightedly with his red, swollen eyes and smiled diffidently as he located Kahnee. The other was Joseph Kenebeg --called by his tribe "The Snake"-- who was disliked and feared by all the other Indians because he could not be trusted. He was staring with hard, glittering eyes at the young Waubegoon, and as he stared, his head constantly turned with a weaving motion from side to side, and his long red tongue kept shooting out from between his thin lips as though he were wetting them. It was on account of these reptilian motions he had received his name. Big John's worry returned again, yet it was against his code of ethics to interfere until there was something tangible to speak of. For the first time Big John realized how beautiful Waubegoon was, with her dusky hair and delicate features, and graceful, slim body. She was appropriately called his "Flower." Impulsively he walked over to the Very Oldest Mother. They all knew she had a clear perspective because she had almost reached the end of her Trail of Life. Big John would have liked to question her and ask if she had any fear of the Black, and what lay beyond the End's Edge, but could not bring himself to betray to her that he was worried or doubtful. However, from her long experience with men-children, the old woman knew. She looked up at him, removed the pipe from her mouth and asked calmly and directly, "What troubles you, Big John? Is it your favorite, Waubegoon?"

"I do not know, Oldest Mother," Big John answered, as simply as a child would. "I am sick in my mind about many things in life which I cannot mend. I need the help and wisdom of the ancient ones, and the old magic, but do not know where to go. Therefore I must use what knowledge I already possess and act according to our customs and traditions. You must have heard that she is promised to someone we trust, Oldest Mother. Has Kenebeg spoken to Waubegoon since she came to the woods today?"

The Very Oldest Woman nodded her head, and tapped the dottle from her pipe against her knee. "Yes, because he desires her. But do not worry about Waubegoon, Big John. Since when have Indian men been even infinitesimally concerned about their women or girl-children! She is beautiful as the lithe young tamarack, but I believe she is yet only a child in mind and body. She dreams a child's dreams of someone who charms her because he is different from the commonplace men she has known. I say they are but child-dreams, though girl-dreams lead to woman-desire so languorously that, like blue sky and blue lake under a hot sun, one cannot always tell when they merge. Aih-ah, Big John, she is filled with youthful fancies, which pass, along with youth and beauty and the thirteen-moon years. Worry no longer, for the tribe needs your mind clear of fretting."

Big John looked into the deep, black, fathomless eyes, and somehow felt consoled, as if his mother had patted his head.

"Our plans still are that she shall marry with Fred Mokok," he confided, "and we shall insist that she keeps her promise to him. Fred builds the best boats, for which he gets more money than any other Indian on the Island. And his arrows and bows are famous with the tourists, who demand them in greater quantities than one man may make, even with hard labor. He is gentle, and will be good to her as, we have always been. I shall not be content unless she is happy."

Kenebeg heard their voices, looked up at Big John, and slipped away through the trees. The Very Oldest Woman laughed soundlessly, and there was something of malice in her expression as she watched him go without a word of farewell. Dusk was already gathering in the thick woods, and black shadows were creeping close. The Very Oldest Mother rose and folded her canvas into a small package. Then she turned again to Big John. Her eyes seemed to have sunk back into her head. Big John wondered if there were any truth in the prevailing belief that Kenebeg was her son. She interrupted his musing and her voice was as soft as the whisper of the small night wind as she advised him. She was withdrawn and secret.

"The moon is at the full tonight, Big John, and the time is right just when you need it so. And you have never asked for assistance at the Place of the Old Ones."

"I have never had need, Oldest Mother," he replied, "and I am not a woman, wanting the stars."

The Very Oldest Woman's voice took on a prophetic tone.

"You have need now, Big John," she suggested. "And times come when we all should reach for stars. Go to the Place tonight, Big John, and as you wait to make your wish you will learn much that you should know as Head of the Tribe."

Without another word, almost as if she had forgotten that she had spoken to him, she turned and left him, and just as silently did Big John leave also, not speaking to Jennie or Waubegoon. Surprised, they leaned on their axes and watched him out of sight. Waubegoon turned to Jennie. "Do you think he knows, Jennie?" she asked anxiously. "Did the Very Oldest Mother tell him, think you?"

Jennie laughed. "No," she said, but there was a real fear underlying her assumed scorn. "They say she knows everything, but how could she know what only you and I do? That is only old people's talk. And they are all so sure you are to marry with Fred Mokok. I do not know what Fred may do when he discovers that his plans will come to nothing, for he is vengeful when he believes he has cause. "She laughed again, and patted her young sister's hand. "No one knows but ourselves," she assured Waubegoon again. "No one _could_ know."

Big John did not go to the store as he had planned. The Very Oldest Woman had reminded him of help which was available to him always, and for everyone; a help which he had almost forgotten was obtainable, and which had all the enchantment and mysticism of old legends behind it. He had never made the one wish each member of the tribe was granted at the Place. Should he make it now, knowing he could never have another? He again stepped off the trail to a big stump, and sat there in the soft dusk, trying to decide what was best to do. After a long time of questioning the wisdom of the advice the Very Oldest Woman had offered, he decided. Coming back to the trail he told the first man he met to tell Mrs. Big John that he might not be home until very late in the night.

Back in the center of the Island was the little natural clearing in the woods, where the Wishing Place was located. The Place was one of mysticism for the Indians. A background of night-mysterious forest was edged with dainty silver poplars which were lighted with an elfish, eerie glimmer by a rapidly rising moon. Slightly to one side of the clearing was a circle of spruce trees, perfect except where two were missing to form an entrance to the ring. Here, for countless generations, had dwelt the Spirit which granted to those who came with unquestioning faith, one wish, if it were not for material possessions or wealth. After a wish was made in the circle, the person must never again enter it, or "bad medicine" would be put upon him by the Spirit.

Big John waited cautiously in the shadow of the encircling woods to see if anyone else had come before him. He did not want any member of the tribe watching him when he went into the Place to make his wish. As he stood there, waiting for the moon to climb high enough in the south so that its rays would fall upon the white stone where the wish was to be spoken, he was amazed to see Kenebeg cross the open space to the entrance of the circle and peer in. Then he heard him laugh softly, and for just a second he turned his head back so he seemed to be staring directly at Big John. Big John shivered as he imagined he saw Kenebeg's eyes glow greenly in the moonlight. Then he slid in and under the low-spreading spruce branches and was hidden from Big John's sight as though he had somehow fused into and become part of their thick, black shadow. And now Big John was further startled to hear voices coming toward him. He drew back deeper into the cover of the woods as he recognized Waubegoon and Jennie. Waubegoon was speaking, and there was a grown-up seriousness in her voice of which Big John would not have believed it capable. He was shocked by the realization that despite the assurances of the Very Oldest Mother, his little Waubegoon was dreaming woman-dreams. She stood at the rim of the clearing, also waiting for the moon rays to light the mysterious, square stone. Her little-girl garland of wilted flowers drooped across the front of her dress. Big John knew she was scared and wanting to go home. She was as elfin as a tree-spirit as she waited there, nervously fingering her flower-chain, and his throat hurt with his great desire to speak to her consolingly.

"Aih-ah, Jennie." she said, "I am afraid of this desire-haunted Place. So many women of our tribe have wished here, and what has come to them? When their wish was granted by the Spirit, was it truly what they would have wished after they had been made wiser by the granting of it? I wonder if the Spirit laughs to himself as he gives us our wish! The thing I want most deeply I cannot say in words, and our thought-wishes are not heard. Only the spoken words can carry our desire to that upper Place where lives the Spirit. Had I better ponder my wish until the next moons Jennie?"

Jennie's answer was a strange, sneering laugh, so unlike her, so hard and brittle that her father crossed himself as he heard. "Those same words you say at every moon. I will not come again with you if you fail to wish this time. And look! The moon's light now falls upon the stone, and the ear of the Spirit is turned to Earth when the light so falls. There is no one here, so hasten in and make your wish without further cowardly faltering, or the light will pass over and it will then be too late. I shall wait for you here at the edge, but you must hurry!"

Waubegoon went into the circle with a certain fearful boldness at Jennie's urging. Big John watched without realizing he was spying. What was it all about! These two girls of his seemed like strange women. Was Jennie somehow jealous of Waubegoon's loveliness? And what was Kenebeg doing there, listening! He saw Waubegoon circle the stone three times. A quick little wind rustled the spruce branches, and as he heard their audible singing whisper, Big John turned his face away, overwhelmed with an unbearable foreboding. At that moment, with all the fortitude of his race, Big John relinquished his hopes of many years, for happiness for Waubegoon. But he had to look again. Waubegoon was kneeling behind the stone, and her earnest face was lighted with the moon's reflection from the whiteness of it, creating the impression of light rays playing about her soft, loosened hair. She placed her slender hands, palms up, flat on the stone and talked with uplifted sensitive face, as though to an Ear, listening. Big John groaned as he heard the wishing chant. How could he have dreamed she was yet a child in her desires! Her voice came monotonously through the singing of the spruce trees, as if she were striving through unaccustomed anguish and tears to remember each word of the ritual.

"Kind Spirit, good Spirit,
Hearken unto my wish,
My first wish, my one wish, ---

Here her voice broke and for a moment he was hopeful, that she would not continue. Then she went on.

> "Which besieges thy Ear.
> Underneath this shining moon,
> I, a maiden, Kneel,
> I kneel in faith
> And play three to grant
> This wish I wish of Thee.
> Thy magic is powerful
> I kneel low in faith,
> My wish, my desire
> Is of loved one and love.
> May he smile on me
> When next we meet."

She removed her hands from the stone as if she had heard some startling sound and would arise, then suddenly, and rather pitifully, it seemed to her father, she bent her head low upon her hands, again placed flat on the stone, and implored wildly and unceremoniously; "Aih-ah, Spirit kind, Grant that he <u>love</u> me."

Big John felt that he could endure it no longer, but as he was about to go to her, Jennie called. "Waubegoon, come now. Your wish is made and you must not remain in the circle." She put her arms around Waubegoon as she came out of the Place. "Don't weep so, Waubegoon. Your wish is already granted, you know, as soon as you utter it. Though you should mourn for all the years of your life-span, you cannot withdraw it now."

Big John could not hear Waubegoon's reply, for the girls walked rapidly across the clearing and into the woods. From under the low branches of the spruce trees, close to the earth, appeared the face of Kenebeg. Big John had an impression that it belonged there, had been there since time began, close to the earth. He writhed out from his hiding place and stood swaying from side to side, shaking loose needles from his clothing. Then he turned in the direction in which the girls had disappeared and grinned evilly, malevolently, while his restless tongue ran rapidly in and out wetting his lips. Big John knew that he actually heard in the silence only the rustling spruce needles, but as the tongue of Kenebeg moved so rapidly, there seemed to come to his ears the faint sound of hissing. For the first time he understood why the others of the tribe hated and feared Kenebeg. As the Snake came toward him, Big John stepped out in front of him, and Kenebeg turned like a flash and faced him. Big John clenched his huge fists in his pockets so he could not be tempted to kill the Snake. As he saw the wicked light in Big John's eyes, Kenebeg began to retreat. Big John kept pace with him. "Kenebeg," he said, and no one had ever heard that thin, deadly quality which had come into his voice, "if ever I discover you spying again upon my daughters, or interfering in any fashion with either of them, I shall kill you,"

Kenebeg did not answer, but Big John imagined that his eyes again shone repulsively green in the moon's light, and his thin, red tongue darted in and out between his lips. Others were coming to wish. Big John could hear laughter and voices. Some of the girls were taunting a few young fellows, who answered with jeers. He looked at the flat stone, shining enticingly, shook his head helplessly and stumbled off into the woods, saying to himself, "Some other time when the need is greater! Another time, when worse things have come!"

CHAPTER V
WAUBEGOON

SYMBOL OF A MAN WALKING AT NIGHT

WAUBEGOON

The Spirit of the Wishing Place must have been favorably impressed with Waubegoon, for just two months later her wish was granted. The days were long and the delicate twilight colors lingered until very late in the evening. Waubegoon left the cabin as the sinking sun reflected rose-lights from the lake to the silver birches, and did not invite Kahnee or Jennie to accompany her. That in itself was odd, for she and Jennie were ordinarily inseparable companions. Jennie was washing dishes, and apparently did not see that her sister was leaving. When Mrs. Big John perfunctorily asked Waubegoon where she was going, she replied quite as casually that she was walking out on the trail, probably as far as the store, to buy some dye for her "timber." There was nothing unusual about her desire for different coloring from that her mother and the other two girls used, for Waubegoon was never contented with their soft browns, greens, blues and yellows. She wanted the most vivid hues she could create for her baskets, and she combined these colors with such consummate skill and sense of harmony that her baskets usually sold far sooner than did those more modestly-tinted ones of the family. Her mother did wonder a little when the girl came into the living room and stared down at her affectionately when she should have been starting on her way if she hoped to return before night fell. But Waubegoon was unlike any other child in the family, and was almost like a white girl in her thinking and reactions, they often thought, taking pride in that fact. They had never been able to understand her or her savage rebellions against the things they had always accepted as a natural part of their lives. They had long ago decided that this difference had been the result of her association with the French girls in the Settlement, for she had been invited often to visit in their homes, and had been intimate since her childhood with several families there. From this contact with white people she had developed covetousness for ways of living that were not for Indians.

Now she grinned at her mother, and, almost too swiftly, left the room. Mrs. Big John looked out from the low window by which she sat weaving in the dim light, and watched her walking slowly down the trail. Mrs. Big John had to smile at her laziness. Waubegoon was such an odd combination of swift impulse and lazy movement. When she came to the wide-spreading oak at the turn of the path, she looked back once and raised her hand high in the Indian gesture of parting, as she noticed her mother watching her. Mrs. Big John smiled again at this characteristic dramatic pantomime of Waubegoon's, but had a queer feeling that the girl tossed her head as though shaking tears from over-filled eyes. Then she laughed quietly at her own foolishness, for Waubegoon seldom cried. She went into sudden, wicked tantrums; she laughed often and immoderately; but weeping was not a part of her character. Her temper had the swiftness of summer gales with their aftermaths of peace. Later, when her own eyes were swollen from long weeping, Mrs. Big John wished fervently that she had spoken to the child before she left the house.

The black summer night wrapped about the cabin and they lighted the lamps, but Waubegoon did not come home. Mrs. Big John sent Kahnee down the trail several times to see if she were coming, for Waubegoon had always hated and feared the night. Finally Big John came from the strange Woman's cabin, where he had been cutting wood for her. He had seen Red-Cow wandering along in the woods and had brought her home with him, but he did not mention that he had seen Waubegoon, either in the Settlement or on the trail. She often visited some of the girls who came part way with her afterward, so the family sat talking on the stoop and waited. At midnight, Big John gave in to his strange uneasiness about her and went out to find her. He walked as far as the store, but the building was dark. The Vargattes were long ago in bed, and of course she was not there with them. Mrs. Vargatte would have sent Armand to tell them and ask their permission if she had invited Waubegoon to stay the night, as she frequently did, for she did not approve at all of the entire lack of discipline and the too-great freedom the Indians allowed their children from the time they were weaned. She had repeatedly remonstrated with Big John about what she termed their carelessness with their girls, especially one as beautiful as Waubegoon, but Big John had only laughed at her.

Neither Waubegoon nor Delima ever told Big John that the girl had actually stopped at the store that night. She had not wanted to go there, but it had seemed that she must talk with someone who was interested in her, and at the same time she must not admit what she was planning to do. She was not deliberately wishing to be deceitful, but she was miserably indecisive. She had admired and loved Mrs. Vargatte always. She had asked if the new dye had been brought down with the supplies from town, and then told Armand, who waited upon her, that she would not buy it after all, but would stop for it the following day. Mrs. Vargatte immediately noticed her hesitance, also that the girl was leaving through the rear door to escape observation, and invited her to come in the living room and visit with her. This Waubegoon was afraid to do, though she longed to talk with this French woman who was really fond of her. She was fearful she would betray herself and might be persuaded to abandon her plan. She was unhappy because Mrs. Vargatte did not know this intuitively, and would have felt more wretched if she had known. She was wrenched in two directions by an instinctive reticence and a desire for encouragement and sympathy. She did not want council, for her mind was determined on the thing she intended to do. She stood on the back porch of the store and talked disconnectedly, hardly knowing what she said. As she stood, listening to Waubegoon in the gray twilight and wondering at her sudden and unnatural volubility, Delima dimly heard from some far place those deep organ notes which always warned her that her friends were in distress. She placed her hand caressingly upon the girl's shoulder. "Tell me, Waubegoon! What troubles you tonight?"

When she saw tears running on Waubegoon's cheeks she became positive there was something terribly amiss. She, too, knew that the girl did not weep easily. "Won't you then tell your oldest friend?" she asked, but Waubegoon could only shake her head. Mrs. Vargatte put an arm about her and pulled her close. "Are you ill, cherie? You are yet a too-young child to be suffering about anything! I would help so gladly, Waubegoon, for I love you. You know that! Do not let me perhaps always feel regret that you could not confide your trouble to me."

She felt that Waubegoon was stiff and unresponsive to her embrace, but before she freed her she held the girl's face in both hands and looked deep into her eyes, and in them she saw such conflict and that her heart was sore with her sympathetic sorrow.

She realized then that even a sincere love could not break down the barrier of race. Quickly she bent down and kissed the girl, then released her. As she felt for that short moment Mrs. Vargatte's kiss, it seemed to Waubegoon that she was walking through a woods in bright daylight, and a smooth, firm-textured maple leaf had brushed her lips. But she shook her head again, smiled through her tears at Mrs. Vargatte and went out and down the trail. Mrs. Vargatte called a goodnight to her, but Waubegoon turned and once again gave the Indian gesture of farewell. Mrs. Vargatte had the queer feeling that Waubegoon was deliberately walking out of the life of her own family. Later in the evening, Theophile asked Delima why she was so worried and restless, and she could give him no definite reason. Her reply that she had heard organ tones caused him to laugh with her in scoffing fashion.

When Big John saw the unlighted windows in the store he made the rounds of all the homes to which Waubegoon might have gone, and found them all dark and silent. Certainty of what had happened grew upon him, but finally he knocked at the door of Mary Shaganaubegon's cabin, which was last on his list of places the girl might have stayed. Mary answered his knock, rubbing heavy sleep from her eyes. "W'at you are wanting?" she asked in English, then recognizing Big John, she repeated her question in Indian.

"Is our Waubegoon here?" he asked, but even as he spoke the words he knew she was not, or Mary would have known what he wanted. He was forced to acknowledge openly his intuition of what had happened.

"No, Big John, Waubegoon has not been here for many weeks. She has avoided all her friends lately. I saw her tonight walking down the trail when I returned from the store late, and she was unknowing that I was taking the same trail. But I felt no anger toward her, for she was walking with that gay fanfaron who lives down the Island."

She was telling him the obvious, and she knew it, but she dreaded to have a moment of silence come between them. There was a malevolence in his face that she feared.

"Did you overhear any of their talk?" He looked at her keenly, reading her face disconcertingly, for he knew she was Waubegoon's most loyal friend and would lie for her without qualms.

"They were not speaking." He knew she was telling the truth. "They were walking fast; going somewhere in a great hurry, and their eyes could see only each other."

"Say nothing about this," Big John commanded, and his face was flint-hard and expressionless again, she nodded, and as he turned off down her trail he heard the door close and the bolt slide into place. There was a time when no bolts were necessary on the Island, he thought disconnectedly. Then Mary's light disappeared, and he knew she had returned to bed and her interrupted sleep.

When he could no longer see the yellow glimmer of her lamp and he was solitary on the path, the same sensation of nausea came again to him that he had known when he had seen his girls at the Wishing Place and had realized they were grown women. He turned from Mary's path to the well-beaten road down to the far end of the Island, and though he had not often traveled this road recently, because it led to that section where all the "outlanders" had settled, his speed was rapid.

He had never seen the rough new shanty which belonged to the alien people, but he knew the location from hearsay. Finally he reached the small cleared space where the cabin squatted low on the ground. No light was in this house either, but he had a lightning suspicion that someone was waiting for him, listening close to the door for his coming. He knocked. He heard stirring in the shack but they kept him waiting, there at the door. He would not go away and knocked again and again. After a long time the door opened just a crack, and a middle-aged, evil-faced woman poked her head out into the dimness, close to Big John, and the odor which came with her made him recoil, involuntarily. Behind her the room seemed intensely black, and as the light from the candle she held high in her hand shone on her face, she seemed to him like an aged witch-woman, for her hair streamed crazily about her head, and he saw she was a misproportioned and humpbacked crone. "Pequahgung," said Big John to himself, then before the woman had time to question him, he asked sharply, "Is your son here?"

The woman sniggered, "He's asleep," she lied and Big John felt that her voice was as ugly as her face.

"Then you will get him to wake," Big John said, and his tone commanded obedience even from this hag, who had controlled men since the time she had been twelve years old. She attempted to close the door as she withdrew into the shanty, but Big John held it open and entered behind her. The candle light went out, so quickly that Big John could not determine whether the woman had extinguished it or a draft had blown it out. "Stand still there, Injun, until I strike a light," she yelled. "You'll knock agin the table and bust my dishes.

He heard her cross the room, and then ensued a silence as deep as though she had vanished through some other noiseless door. Big John felt trapped, as he always did in a strange shut-in place, and this he could not endure. "Hurry with that light," he called across the blackness, "or this table will be over-knocked. I come, me!"

There came from the other side of the room the sound of a match being scratched over a rough board wall, and he saw the small flare as it caught and lighted. The woman moved toward the table and touched the match to the wick of the kerosene lamp sitting there. The room opened up dimly to Big John's view as the lamp burned. He noted unconsciously that the woman still leaning toward the lamp had unnatural, gold-finch-colored hair, which seemed strangely grotesque above her wrinkled and scarred face. He wondered how such an ugly-formed woman could ever have attracted men.

Behind the woman, in her tall, weird shadow, stood her bright-haired son, and even in that moment of strain, Big John had to admit honestly to himself that the lad was handsome enough to attract any girl, even though his mouth was thin and cruel. He was fully dressed and Big John knew he had not been asleep. Then, with an almost unbearable grief in him, Big John saw that beside this man stood Waubegoon, shielding her face with her arm as though she could not endure looking at her father. What was most indicative to him was the fact that with her other hand she clutched the coat of the alien, who stood close to her. Though he felt a peculiar dizziness and discovered that he had lost the wickedness of his anger somewhere on the lonesome trail down to this place, Big John stood as solidly as the oak in his own yards and looked straight at her. For what seemed a very long time not one word was spoken. They were all measuring each other. When Waubegoon finally raised her eyes to him, as though he had somehow forced her despite her stubborn will, Big John said, as placidly as if they two were alone in the room, "Your mother has wondered why you did not come home, Little Flower. Will you come with me now and relieve her great worry?"

Waubegoon turned her gaze away, and now the man moved forward within range of the light rays and spoke for the first time to Big John. As he talked he stared intently at the huge Indian, and his eyes were intensely blue. "I don't understand your Injun gibberish, so I don't know what you're sayin' to her, and I don't give a damn either, for I know she won't listen to you. She's plumb crazy about me, and she's the best-lookin' woman on the Island, even though she's straight Injun. She's stayin' right here, and you'd better let that idea sink in. You Injuns allus let your let kids do what they want, so now get out and leave her alone."

Big John ignored him as though he were some inanimate thing standing there so blusteringly. Persuasively he spoke to his beloved child as if she were yet that Little Flower they had petted and spoiled. "Come, Small One. The night is getting old, and at home they are greatly concerned about you. We have a long walk ahead of us. Get your coat now and come with me. Tomorrow we will unsnarl all this tangled weaving."

Waubegoon remembered from babyhood that coaxing note in his voice as he had soothed her when she was afraid of the dark, and she could not answer him. Mrs. Crash giggled. Big John felt such a loathing of her sweep over him that again he became sick.

"She ain't goin' with you," said the young fellow. "She's promised she'd live here with me just as long as I want her."

"Aw, shut up, Bill, and let's see what she'll do," advised the old harridan, and grinned because she knew now they would win. "It's fun to hear them p'laver in that blasted lingo." She hated the girl to as great a degree as she adored her son. Later, when Bill had become weary of her evanescent prettiness, she would make her step lively, but this present situation satisfied her innate cruelty and she was having pleasure from the conflict of wills.

Even now Big John apparently did not notice that anyone else was in the room. He went close to her and placed his hand on Waubegoon's shoulder. She winced away from the gentle touch. His hurt became deeper. Never had Waubegoon been afraid of him. But his voice was steady and deep, and more solemn than usual. The girl knew what he was feeling and was drawn to him against her will.

"Come, Waubegoon. Come home with me to your mother. She has been sick, as you know, and is not yet cured. This worry is not good for her.

Waubegoon reached for Bill's hand and clung to it. Then she stared defiantly at her father. "I am not coming," she said. "In the Place I wished Bill would smile at me, and he has done more. He has said that he wants me, and I shall stay with him always."

Big John stared at her unbelievingly. The woman laughed derisively, and pushed the hair from her eyes, the better to see what was happening.

"Tell my mother I am staying here," Waubegoon screamed suddenly, hysterically. "I cannot help myself and what I now do. I am staying because I cannot leave him again." She ran from the room into another adjoining one and slammed the door shut against her father.

For a moment Big John stood, stricken and uncomprehending. Then, with his face betraying to these aliens no emotion of any kind, he swung around and went out of the house. When the door closed behind him, the mother and Bill looked at each other. "So that's the heap big Injun Chief! I allus knew Injuns hadn't no gumption," Bill remarked, but his voice was off-key with his relief." That was a cinch!"

Mrs. Crash giggled at him. "It wouldn't of been so damned easy if the girl hadn't been so set to stay. But that's what them Injuns get for lettin' their kids have their own way. Damn spoiled brats!"

Again she blew out the light. "Let it stay out," she cautioned, and leered at her son meaningfully. "Then if he changes his mind and comes back he mebbe won't bother us no more" When he first come in he almost had me buffaloed."

She climbed up into the upstairs room, and Bill went into the room where Waubegoon was waiting. But Big John did not change his mind. Waubegoon had made her choice and her decision was final. As he went home he wondered what he could tell Mrs. Big John so her disappointment would not be too great. Her illness had left her weak, and Waubegoon was her best-loved child. He was weary as he never had been before. He even stumbled at times over small, up-sticking roots in the path, for this night seemed darker than any night he had known. And though the month was early July, the odor of dead, moulding leaves came constantly to his nostrils. He had relinquished his own plans for her when he saw Waubegoon wishing at the Place, but now his wife had to be wounded by him as a result of failure with the girl. That was harder than his own grief. He remembered Theophile Vargatte's jeers at the folks who were so busy settling the affairs of others that they had no time to take care of their own. Was that his dilemma?

He began to feel as if he were dreaming a horrible nightmare, in which he was walking endlessly, without sound or feeling, into a blank space, and he could not keep his thoughts on this tragedy that had happened to his child. He was almost light-headed and his mind skipped from one inane idea to another with unwonted agility, despite his resolution to decide upon an easy way to break the news to his wife. He wondered if, when one stepped over the End's Edge and into the Darkness of Death, one stumbled so unsurely and tripped so often as he followed the Black Trail. Why had he begun questioning and wondering what lay beyond death now, when such thoughts had never bothered him, and were entirely outside the problem he was deciding! And was death like this? A going out from a lighted cabin, which one left unwillingly even though he had been grievously hurt by life, into a darkness of oblivion so solid that there seemed to be not one ray of light! He was glad beyond all reasonableness to see the High Light flaring out over the water, as the trail swung east and wound along the shore. He felt there was not another living person in the world. He was isolated in a huge ball of black night, through which nothing moved but the Light, regularly flashing its signal to the lake boats. Again he questioned. Was death as lonesome a thing as this experience he was having? Did one feel so queerly desolate even on his path to the Happy Islands where all those of the tribe who had gone ahead were waiting? At that moment he saw the light in his own cabin. Again he became practical, his thoughts were under control, and he returned them to Waubegoon and what he must explain to his wife.

When she heard him coming up on the stoop, Jennie opened the door for him, and the light shone full upon his face. Immediately she knew Waubegoon had done what they had planned she should do, and that he knew her share in bringing it about, yet was not censuring her even though she had fallen mightily in his esteem and affection. He dropped his hat on the stand near the door and went swiftly to Mrs. Big John, where she sat by the stove, her huge body huddled in the big rocker, flaccid and helpless. She looked at her husband, and Jennie felt like an outsider when she saw what was in her mother's eyes. She was abashed and motioned to Kahnee to come with her out of the room and leave the two alone together, but Big John stopped them with a gesture. So they sat and waited until he could speak, and when they realized he was groping for the easiest words, Kahnee, the stolid, dependable one, who seemed more Indian than any of them, reached over and stroked her mother's hand, with an unusual demonstration of feeling.

After a time Big John told them all he knew. He described for them exactly what had happened in the outlander's shanty and advised what the future attitude of the family should be with Waubegoon. Jane Big John was quietly weeping as he concluded with solemn finality, "The Trail of our Waubegoon led her down into a deep valley. Just now she does not foresee the darkness and the ugly shadows which wait there for her; she stands on the high brink, from which she cannot see what lies below. It is hidden from her. I tried to coax her to step back with us and walk our Trail a little longer, but she would not. It might possibly be that she could not, as she said. Now she will go with strange people, and we realize her path may never again meet ours. We must let her go, for that is Life. Yet if her Trail once again joins ours when she crosses her valley, then must we all walk with her in understanding and peace as we always have done. There must be no harsh words spoken, or reproaches. Do not weep, Mother. All Trails merge at the End, and she may sometime return to us." He placed his hand over hers where it lay inertly on the arm of the rocker.

Now, again, Jennie glanced at Kahnee, and Kahnee nodded. They tried hard not to make any sound as they crept up the squeaking stairs to their bedroom. As they climbed the last steps they looked down over the balustrade into the living room, and noticed that Big John had pulled his chair even closer to the rocker, where their mother sat with her head now bowed low on her breast. Even as they gazed, his arm moved up and across her shoulder protectively, and remained there. She groaned hopelessly and did not move, but somehow she seemed comforted and strengthened. The girls entered their own room and did not know that their parents sat hand in hand, sometimes talking in low tones, sometimes saying nothing, but sharing this, their newest and worst sorrow, until the dawn light crept through the windows of the shabby living room. Circles of color began to appear on the floor, strewn with coiled basket "timber"; blue, green, purple, brown, orange, Waubegoon's discarded gay reds and brilliant yellows. The day grew brighter.

When Big John knew that at last his wife slept, with her head sagging wearily against the side of the chair-back, the sun was shining.

CHAPTER VI
WHITE-TIPPED ARROW

SYMBOL OF MAGIC SKILL WITH ARROW

THE WHITE-TIPPED ARROW

One dull yellow day in October, Mary Shaganaubegon came over to see how Mrs. Big John was feeling. She had been very ill again after Waubegoon had gone away with Bill Crash. There were many things to be discussed in detail and Mary loved to gossip. In September Jennie had gone down to the Indian School in the southern part of the state, and Mary wished greedily to know if the school was all that Jennie had imagined it to be, and how Joe Pete had reacted to her arrival there. Young John had departed for the dredge, as had been planned, but he had been sent farther on where men were measuring the depth of the water for a new channel. Jim would soon be leaving for Canada and the wood-camps, where Young John would join him when the dredge was forced to lay up for the winter. Abe was working in the store after school hours, and was staying at Vargatte's at night, since Armand had gone to the seminary in Montreal to become a priest. The strange Woman was quite puzzled because Deneece was learning to walk, and Mary had had to explain to her that all babies walked as soon as their legs grew strong enough to hold them up. They laughed at her vivid word-sketches, but the Big Johns knew that she had come with the definite purpose of telling some important piece of news. They did not hurry her, however, and talked of trivial incidents until she was ready to disclose what she had heard.

Finally Mary, quite deliberately, told them that Fred Mokok had returned to the Island. He had been working all summer at a camp for boys, which was located on a larger island a few miles away. It was a luxurious place for some wealthy families. They came from the big cities, and had unlimited money to satisfy every desire or caprice they might have. The Indians had been told that white people all over the country were making a fad of arrow shooting, which they called archery. So Fred Mokok, the expert, had been hired at this expensive camp to make his wonderful bows and arrows, and teach the boys some of his skill in shooting. Now the camp had been closed for the season, Mary said, and Fred had helped with the last-minute work. He had been home at least a week. This worried the Big Johns, for Fred was their closest neighbor and friend, and their plans had been that he was to marry Waubegoon the next year, when he had built his new house. Because he had needed money to buy lumber, he had taken the job at the camp, and while he had been gone, Waubegoon had chosen another man. Though Big John had hoped that would make no difference in their friendship with Fred, he had had misgivings, and the fact that Fred had not come to visit them proved that his forebodings were not without a foundation. Usually theirs was the first place he visited after an absence from the Island. When Mary discovered that they had not known any of this, she added that folks said Fred had gone nowhere since his arrival, not even to the store, but sat morosely at home, with his door closed against all chance visitors. After Mary went home that night, Big John decided he would go over and visit Fred the next day.

However, the following day Big John did not go anywhere, not even to town with the mail; nor for a week could anyone travel on the Island without getting muddled and lost. Overnight a fog had descended upon them, and none knew if it had risen from the lake or dropped upon them from the sky. One moment it was not there and the next moment it was with them, so thickly opaque that one could not see ahead of him the length of his own outstretched arm. The Islanders had never seen such a fog, nor had one similar ever been described, even by the most aged Indians. They could feel no movement of the air; it was as still as the stagnant bog. Their ears were tortured by the continuous fog-whistles from the freighters, and the sound was so twisted and muffled that one could not locate its source until he almost stumbled into the lake.

Each day they believed the fog cloud must disappear again, but each day it seemed to become more dense, like a blanket of dirty gray velvet hung between their world and the sun. Huge thick rolls of it crawled like ghostly, fabled serpents around their cabins and through the forest, until trails became dim and impossible to follow. When night came it brought with it only a deeper degree of darkness. The moonlight came thinly through that mist-curtain and was a hazy beam of liquid. Great drops of water seemed to hang suspended in the atmosphere, wetting them to the skin in a moment, and clogging the air so that they could breathe it with difficulty, and it had a peculiar odor of brown bogs, of fish, old dampness, dead leaves and rotting wood, all blended into one. When Big John called to Jim, who had gone down toward the dock to feed his tame muskrats, his voice seemed to drop and fall flat at his own feet. The Indians were convinced that the fog was an evil omen and would not leave their houses; and after a week of the darkness and intense discomfort, the white population had much of the same feeling. All activity stopped and the only sounds were the echoes of the boat whistles, frantically warning each other of their whereabouts, until finally they were forced to drop anchor and the ringing of their bells then became stationary.

Just as suddenly as it had come, it disappeared one morning when they came to their doors, the fog was gone and the sun shone from a sky of intense blue. And that very day, after Big John had made his trip up to the town and had delivered the mail to the store, he went over to Fred's cabin. However, he went with a feeling that was a hang-over from the fog, for he had been scared too, though Telesphore had grinned at him and said that some wise person could explain it all quite easily.

Fred lived in the small log hut that his father had built when he had made the clearing long ago. It was raised above the earth and was banked with mud which was held in place by old, time-blackened boards. At one side of the hut was a huge stump, and on this Fred had fastened a target. About the dooryard was a weathered litter of shavings, split logs and narrow strips of cedar and ash. Against the whitewashed walls leaned a long-bow. A fresh pile of yellow chips told Big John that Fred was home and was working again. From a basket beside the door, bright-colored feathers whirled about in the breeze which had blown the fog away, and the ground was amber-carpeted with soggy fallen leaves.

When Big John hailed him, Fred came to the door. Contrary to his usual habit he did not invite Big John into the house or offer him some tobacco, instead he lowered himself to the door-sill and motioned Big John to seat himself on a huge square timber drawn up close. Big John saw that Fred held a number of partly-finished arrows, ready for feathering, and one of these had a head of stone, mistily transparent and beautiful. It was a perfect heart-shape, and Big John idly wondered where Fred had obtained the piece of stone, for he had never seen one similar. Then he realized that Fred was not speaking, and, as they usually did, he began the conversation with the obvious, to gain time to logicalize his arguments.

"Did you like this camp for boys?"

"Yes?" said Fred. "They were nice boys and eager to learn all I could teach them of the woods, --and shooting."

"No other Indian could teach them so much as you," commented Big John sincerely. "With nothing but a knife you can enter the woods, and soon you will have a bark shelter and any other thing you need."

But Fred did not seem to hear this compliment, which at any other time would have pleased him mightily, coming from Big John, and refused to comment. There was a long-drawn silence. Fred worked at his feathering, sorting the colors as he needed them. He was placing the white feathers in one pile, Big John saw. Occasionally, as he completed an arrow, he stopped working, took the long-bow from the wall, and shot the arrow at the cardboard target. Always it sped to its mark, never missing the center, and quivered there without falling, so deeply had it driven through the target into the stump. He did not retrieve the arrows, but always began on another.

"Did you know Waubegoon had gone from us?" Big John at last questioned, knowing he must face the situation. "She is with Bill Crash, in the new outlander settlement." "That is the thing I have heard," Fred commented, as unemotionally as if they were discussing a stranger, and holding the white-tipped arrow in his hand he squinted at it with his eyes half-closed. "But I was waiting for you, her father, to verify the rumor. She followed him, though she was promised to me long ago, and willingly gave her consent. Could you not stop her, you the great man of authority? And have our women become as vacillating and dishonest as those of the whites?"

"We could not stop her, Fred. We did not comprehend how deep was her feeling for the stranger. She was infatuated. She did not intend dishonesty, and I do not believe she understood her own sudden recklessness. She forgot even the seriousness of a promise. The Outlander must have put a love-spell upon the child."

"She put the spell upon herself," Fred contradicted. "She brought the spell upon herself and it remained with her because she so wantonly desired it to remain. But tell me what you can of it."

As Big John described the scene at the Wishing Place and Kenebeg's actions, and told what had occurred the night he had gone after Waubegoon, Fred began feathering the arrow he held in his hand, with the soft, white feathers he had put aside. Swiftly and skillfully they were placed and bound, then he balanced it across his fingers, stroking every particle of down into slick smoothness. When Big John had finished speaking, Fred did not reply, and Big John found himself staring also, just as intently as the other, at this white-tipped and feathered arrow. After a time Fred spoke, but not to Big John. He had forgotten that Big John was there, and in the Indian language his words were like a chant.

"This is the perfect arrow," he said in monotone. "Magic went into the making of it; charms were crooned over its polishing; beauty is the essence of it; great speed was fashioned into the fiber of it; and never has it missed a mark to which it was sped." Then he flared about at Big John, as though he resented his presence there with him, and now his voice rose and fell in anger. "The whites have everything. They have their own women, and they reach out and snatch ours also. They own much land, but they grasp our little places. We have lost all that fire of strength that ran in swift, biting flame through our forefathers, and we relinquish to them without a murmur whatever they ask of us. In all our poor, sick tribe there's not one man to oppose them."

It was the old complaint of an oppressed tribe, and Big John could not answer it or feel any resentment at Fred's indictment of himself. He shrugged his shoulders as though shaking a load from them and reached out for the arrow Fred held so caressingly in his hand. "Let me look at this perfect arrow," he said. When Fred passed it to him he examined it with interest. The oily-smooth stone tip was as lovely as a carved gem, but keen and thin as a knife blade, and there were two cruelly pointed barbs on each of the curves where they joined the shaft. After it had pierced a body it could not be removed without leaving a terrible and fatal wound. Big John felt the barbs with his blunt finger ends and shivered. They were so sharp, and the arrow, he knew, was wickedly speedy. Fred watched him furtively. Big John sensed his scrutiny, and said trying to keep his voice matter-of-fact. "Our old fathers told that our Iroquois enemy made an arrow that struck with a whirling motion and when it was pulled from its victim, it made a wound like this." He crossed his two first fingers to form an X. "One never recovered from such a wound!"

Fred reached jealously for his arrow. "Telesphore brought me that arrow head from a far-away country where there were, probably three thousand years ago, craftsmen of clever skill. They used magic charms for their weapons, Telesphore says, in this Chinese land, and their arrow heads were the most beautiful in the world. When he saw this one for sale in a market place he bought it for me."

"I do not like it, Fred," Big John criticized bluntly. "Why did those people spend hours polishing and making beautiful a thing designed primarily for killing? It reminds me of the thick fog, white and uncertain, and of sinister omen. Our people made their arrow heads for the purpose, and not for beauty. The charms of these ancient Chinese were always evil, maybe?"

"That I do not know. Telesphore did not say, but I shall question him if he comes here again." Fred spoke quietly now.

Big John was dissatisfied. He did not want to talk of arrows, no matter how unusual they might be. He came back to the subject they were discussing. "You understand, Fred, that we could not undo the evil thing after it had happened? It was her path and she had to walk in it." You do not blame us, or the child?"

He waited for an answer, but Fred sat down again upon the door sill, staring at the white-tipped arrow. He turned his head stubbornly aside, and Big John knew he would not reply. When the silence became monotonous, Big John arose and began to walk away, hoping Fred would call a friendly goodbye to him. He had not gone more than fifty feet from the door when a white streak flashed past his head and struck the target in the exact center of the colored arrows clustered there. He heard the whistling sound of it, but it had hit the tree stump before he could think what was happening, his eyes could focus upon its flight. There it trembled for the fraction of a second, and then dropped to the ground, almost hidden in the honey-colored leaves. Big John knew that Fred had not shot with full force, but had gauged his distance delicately. He turned and looked back at Fred, who had risen and was standing at his full height in the doorway. As Big John swung about, Fred called out to him.

"That is my answer!"

"For him or for her?" Big John demanded.

But when he noticed a cruel, ugly twist to Fred's mouth, he realized he would never know until the event occurred. He went on out of the clearing, knowing that the man he was leaving was not the friend he had been.

Fred returned to his work of feathering his arrows, without picking up the beautiful white one. Little, vagrant pieces of white blew about his head, and he stopped his work and watched them listlessly. One came close to him and he reached swiftly out and caught it with his free hand. He smoothed it between his sensitive fingers and muttered to himself. "They blow about in every slight wind, these first-shed feathers of the young things. Are all young so easily whiffed about, not knowing their own minds? Did Kenebeg, who desires her, perhaps wish that her trail should lead through dark ways, and that I must follow her with my mind because I love her? One could never know what is in his black heart. I could almost wish -----" He opened his fingers and the feather was caught from his palm by a tiny gust of wind and soared upward, higher and higher, until it floated from his sight. Like an entranced child Fred stood watching it, with uplifted face. When Big John turned at the edge of the clearing for one backward glance, he saw Fred standing so, and for no obvious reason felt relieved though he had definitely decided he must warn Waubegoon that her trail should never again meet Fred's if that could possibly be prevented.

Again as he turned to follow the road toward the far end of the Island, though it was daylight and the sun was flickering upon the trees, he fell into aimless thinking. He was only half-conscious of the tangy odor of the jackpines and cedars. Bluejays hailed each other clamorously, and dropped from the higher trees across the trail to the low sumac shrubs, scarlet in the sun. Gray juncos flitted along, close to the ground and as quiet as mice. A partridge went up with a roar of wings as he passed, but he did not see or hear any of this.

When he came within sight of the Outlander's place he saw Waubegoon crossing the yard behind the house, carrying a big pail of water and refuse which she emptied into a hole dug there. She did not see him, even when she straightened and stood with her hand pressing against her side as she rested a moment before returning. She was thin and her lovely brown skin had turned almost a yellow color, she was so wan. Big John knew the Indian women faded rapidly, but he could not understand how there could have been such a change in this child during the few months she had been away from them. He heard Mrs. Crash yell at her from the kitchen door, and Waubegoon stooped wearily and picked up the pail. When she turned she saw her father. Gladness shot across her face, then she glanced furtively toward the house, and stood motionless, waiting for him to come to her. When he reached her he saw that she was terribly fatigued. Perspiration streaked her face and stood in tiny beads above her upper lip. She was a woman, grown up and with a grave demeanor, which removed her farther from them than her actual departure had. She seemed older than her mother in grief and wisdom. Big john spoke to her through a thick throat. "Waubegoon! Little Flower! What has come to you in this place!"

"Why are you here," she questioned, and her voice made him think of a stone out-cropping in a green pasture near their cabin. "You should not come here, to be insulted and laughed at by that humpbacked devil! You know I cannot go home with you. Why do you come! To hurt me?"

"Have you indeed gone so far from us that you ask that?" he said quietly, and she turned away from him so he would not see her wet eyes and pity her more than he already did.

"I do know better, my father, but what I have endured here made me forget for a moment. You must not come here. It only wounds both of us and cannot change .what has happened. I have answered my own question, my father, and I know, with bitter sureness, that the Spirit in the Wishing Place laughs at us futile little humans when he grants our foolish desires."

She shook her head in her old childish gesture of shaking away her tears. "How is my mother? The Very Oldest Woman told me she had been ill again. I have wanted and needed her in the dark night when I was too weary and sleep passed me."

"We were fearful that she would go away from us after you went that night," Big John answered, and even her keenness did not catch any undertone of reproach in his voice. "She loved you more than all the others, Waubegoon. I came, however, not to speak of that, but to warn you and this outlander who took you. Fred Mokok has returned, and he has just finished making an evil, white-tipped arrow of ill omen. It was his right to demand that you must keep your promise to him, or avenge your breaking of it. This has always been the law in our race. Watch constantly on the trails, both of you, and do not meet him. He is silent but---"

Mrs. Crash shrieked again, then came to the door to see what was delaying Waubegoon. When she saw him she grinned, and again Big John loathed her. "Hello, Big Feller," she greeted him insolently. "You come back again, hey whadda you want this time?"

Big John ignored her. "Remember what I have said, Waubegoon."

The woman pushed between them, and the smell of her, as though she were permeated with the odor of half-washed clothing, greasy cooking and long-forgotten dirt, made him sick. He wondered why a dirty white person smelled more nauseatingly than a dirty Indian.

"I don't care what you've said to her, for I know she ain't goin' with you," she shrilled at him. "No such luck for I and Bill. She ain't even earned her board since she come here. She can't do nothin' to help out, and me feedin' twenty men off of the drudge. She just sets around and grumps. I never seen a girl go so sickly before, even though she was goin' to have a brat. And I thought squaws was tough!" When she saw the startled glance Big John stole at Waubegoon, she added spitefully, "She ain't told you, then! It's bad enough to have her here, doi'n nothin', without havin' a baby on our hands too."

Big John turned. "Would you come home now, Waubegoon?"

She can go if she wants to, for alla me. She's no good here, and we're gettin' sick of it."

Waubegoon shook her head at her father.

"Then remember what I said." Though the old hag chortled, he patted Waubegoon on the shoulder, and this time she did not wince beneath his touch. Again she had decided, so there was nothing he could do. He held his hand high in fare-well and walked rapidly away from the place.

When he passed through a low, damp section of his woods, he gathered fungi for Mrs. Big John to put in her flat blue bowl; fragile stemmed fairy white ones, brilliant scarlet ones, brown and tan and yellow ones; and wrapped them carefully inside a sheet of moss which was like elfin ferns massed in layers. Their earthy, elusive fragrance seemed to cleanse his lungs of the hag-odor which had seemed to cling to him.

Jane Big John was sitting out on the stoop, warmly wrapped in a soft shawl. She removed the pipe from her lips and smiled when he came up the steps. Kahnee and Jim grinned at him, confidently. "You were long, Big John. How is Fred, and what did he say?" Mrs. Big John asked quite serenely. If he had remained this length of time with Fred, everything was right. Big John grinned back at them and suddenly the question he had pondered all the way home was decided for him. He would not destroy that peace upon her tired face. She did not need to know of Waubegoon for a time yet, and then she would be stronger and better able to bear the telling.

"He seemed well," he answered them, as if he had just come from Fred's cabin. He was very busy making arrows, beautiful ones of all colors. He has a special order which he must fill. Then we shall see him again."

CHAPTER VII
THE WINTER OF CHANGE

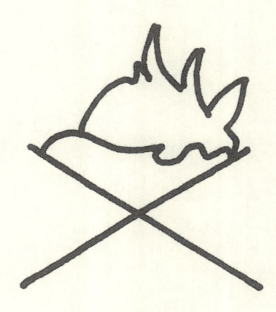

SYMBOL OF AN ENCAMPMENT

THE WINTER OF CHANGE

By the end of November the ice had formed far out, even shelving over the deep, black water, and many fish-shanties were dotted upon its wind-ridged surface. Every night the dark was broken and enlivened by tiny orange lights flickering erratically across the snow, as the younger members of the tribe, both girls and boys, hurried with their lanterns out to their chosen spot for spearing. There was much merriment, and laughing comparisons of the sizes of their catches were the rule. Those whose shanties were not placed over the "run" were chaffed and advised to move. Often, on the still, biting evenings they paused long enough to listen to the startling echoes of their laughter that were returned to them from the hills which rose almost from the shore of the Island.

The ground was deep with early snow, which the old ones predicted would remain all winter, because the earth was hard-frozen before the snow had fallen. They were also foretelling an unusually hard season, for all the trees and shrubs were burdened with fruits, cones and berries. The north-west wind, tearing down from Lake Superior, had a keen, nipping edge, and the people in the Settlement had sealed their log houses against it with their storm windows, and piled great stacks of wood in their sheds. Some of the houses were banked with snow up almost to the eaves. The Canada jays came close to the back doors to forage for the scraps left by the dogs. The High Light burned a few days after the last down-bound boat had passed and then went out. It would not flash again until navigation opened in the Spring. This always marked the period of isolation of the Island from the rest of the world.

The first day of December Telesphore Dinet came over to the Big John cabin to say goodbye, though he had intended staying with the Vargattes all winter. During the years he had been in the city he had longed to spend a winter in the woods, and had anticipated its beauty and romance. But the actual experience was too much for him, he explained to them now, with an embarrassed grin at his spinelessness. He could not endure the bite of the arctic winds since he had become "softened" by spending the winters in warmer climates. He was already weary of wading through piles of snow every time he stepped out of doors, and the unaccustomed weight of snowshoes hampered his freedom of movement. He had forgotten that the monotony of the long-spanned northern winter, the eternal whiteness, the blue and purple shadows and the too-short days had always irked him into a wild restlessness. So he had decided to go to the city until the Spring months came again, when he would return to a more beautiful Island. Big John knew Telesphore had something weighty on his mind because he was quieter than usual. He was more practical than Big John had ever seen him. He insisted that they should pile their wood so it would form a wind-break and keep the snow from drifting across and closing the trail to the cabin. He suggested that they should save themselves both work and worry by bringing the Strange Woman and the Child, Deneece, either to their own cabin, or to one closer than Green-Cloud's, in which she was still living. He seemed to feel that these two were his protégées because he was the only one who could speak the language of the strange Woman. He offered to send to Big John each month a small sum, but one which would assure enough food all winter for the two stray ones. His gestures as he talked were more restrained than was customary, but Big John knew they would all miss Telesphore; his vivacity and mirthfulness, his gentle kindness, almost womanish, his histrionic solemnity and the gleam of his strong white teeth when he smiled. It was true that he was more or less a poseur who always wished to be the center of any group, and habitually made almost any situation dramatic and emotional, but even that quality was an amusing and likeable one when it was Telesphore's.

When they were with Mrs. Big John they talked desultorily for awhile, each cautiously avoiding any serious topic. She laughed at the Half-Breed's comments on what he would do when he returned to the huge city which he called home, and the gifts he would send from there if she would allow him to present her with them. "You will forget old Jane Big John then," she retorted finally in answer to his foolishness, "and your gifts will go to the pretty girls you will find there, especially the Madeline one of whom you speak most often. With you it is that when one is not before your eyes, also he is not remembered."

"I shall prove to you then that you are mistaken," he vowed seriously, "for I shall send to you that dress of the brightest purple color which I shall be able to find." And at their mental picture of Mrs. Big John arrayed in a purple dress, they all laughed together. Telesphore immediately sobered again. "Certain it is," he continued, "that I shall see pretty girls and maybe court and marry with Madeline, that modest, dove-like one, if she will have me. I would wish such a wife as you have been to Big John through the years, through gladness and sorrow, but your like are not to be found in every town. Could I discover one, I would put all my heart into the task of winning her, even to using the old love-charms of the tribe."

They laughed at him, but they knew he was semiserious in what he had said. Finally Telesphore rose to leave, but he could not go away without warning Big John against Fred Mokok, though he felt quite positive that Big John knew the situation better than did anyone else. So he invited Big John to accompany him down the trail a short distance, and, when they shook hands in parting, under the huge-limbed oak which still clung stubbornly to its crisped brown leaves, he spoke solemnly enough.

"Watch with eyes like a fish-hawk's that Fred. One great fool I was to bring for him that white arrow-head as a wedding gift, for it came to me with a strange tale of evil vengeance attached, which I was a yet greater fool to relate to him. He sits too much alone, and thinks, and his eyes are sometimes wicked. If I had known the Flower would never wed with him I would not have given him the arrow. When I just now went there, on my path from the Strange Woman's house, he asked many questions further concerning the story and former use of the arrow-head, which I avoided answering as best I could. Watch him, Big John, my good friend, for those too-quiet ones are ever more wicked than those who rant much. He acts as does a man who is planning something sinister."

"He has become a stranger to us, but I do not think he will do harm to one of us," Big John answered, apparently casually, but a glance, keen and packed with words they would never speak aloud, passed between them.

Telesphore acquiesced, and his smile again flashed out at his friend. "It may be that you are right, Neegee. And that snake-devil, that Joseph Kenebeg, has gone to the camps on the down-river island, I have heard. He will be away during the next four months, and that means there will be no trouble-maker to stir up hatreds and fights in the tribe for you to settle. That should do much to help make the winter pleasant. Often shall I think of you all, and wish you were in the city with me."

He gripped Big John's hand once again in his, then released it and headed down the trail, whistling merrily. "My lover wears a plume of feathers on his head. And a bird --or moth-- flutters to the music of his flute ---"

As Big John stood listening to the rustling leaves above him and watching Telesphore vanish from sight, he thought he had never seen anyone else walk with such a jubilantly jaunty swing as this man. He also rued the fact that there would be no more story-telling around the hot stove on stormy winter nights, with the Half-Breed gone, for he was the natural-born raconteur, and his tales of strange adventures which had happened to him in foreign countries held a whole group intently listening, far into the night. The day seemed just a little empty as he went back into his cabin. True it was that one had friends of all kinds, but one like Telesphore was the sun shining from a clear sky. He followed the suggestion which Telesphore had given him, and the next day fastened a box, big enough to hold the Child, well-wrapped, on the small hand-sled, and went over to Green-Cloud's old cabin. He brought home with him the Strange Woman who, to his surprise, came willingly as with a trusted friend, and Deneece. When they were met at the door by Mrs. Big John and Kahnee, smiling a glad welcome, Big John wondered if he only imagined that the Strange Woman seemed happier. At least she smiled, and appeared to settle in with them as if she had again come to a place which was familiar and a refuge.

Almost from the minute that Big John lifted Deneece from the sled and carried her in to be placed in Mrs. Big John's arms, conditions bettered in their cabin. The un-common quietness which had come after Jim's departure to the winter lumber camps, and Abe's removal to the Vargatte's for the Christmas work, was now lifted. Even for a few days the Strange Woman laughed and tried to converse with them in her incomprehensible tongue, and they believed she was content to be constantly with people again. For this short respite the fear that had haunted her, of Someone standing just behind her or coming down the trail after her, was lessened. She still made the jerking movement of looking back over her shoulder, but it was more because it had become a habit and none of her former terror impelled it.

Deneece, the Child, was beautiful. They loved to watch her crawling slowly about on the floor, walking a few steps at a time on wobbling little feet, making queer sounds and smiling at something invisible to them. They guessed that she was probably fifteen or sixteen months old. Her hair became copper-colored, and was a mass of soft curls which Kahnee brushed gently each day. As she hunched her way about on the floor, her hair seemed to catch all the light in the cabin and hold it focused there. Mrs. Big John sometimes wondered about the Child, for her own children could speak many words when they had been at the age of Deneece, and had also walked fairly well. The Child made no attempt to talk and they did not force or coax her overmuch to make the effort. They would not have done that, even with an Indian baby, and this Child was set apart as an object almost of reverence. Mrs. Big John gave her gaily colored scraps of basket-timber, which had always amused her babies, but they did not hold this Child's attention or interest. She held them slackly with both fists, looked at them with strangely empty eyes, then dropped them again and smiled at everyone impartially. It was not long before the whole household revolved about the Child and her needs. To buy bright ribbons and warm dresses for her, Jane Big John again took up her weaving, and the family was happy to see her at the old familiar task.

Then the big snows began to come. The white piles banked up against the High Light until only the iron crossbars were visible. Day after day the air was completely filled with drifting, swirling white, and the cabin was darkened as if a thick curtain had been hung outside the windows. Mrs. Big John was unconcerned, and sat close by the big window where the light was best, weaving as long as the dim day lasted. Kahnee did not like the snow, because Moses Katemishkid remained home when walking became an effort, but she seemed more the old, stoic Indian than her parents, and did not comment. The Big Johns believed Kahnee was like her great-grandmother for whom she was named. She was cold and aloof with strangers for she knew she was not so handsome as Jennie or Waubegoon. Her smoothly-kept coarse hair was blue-black. Her hands were very large and unbeautifully formed, and she was too conscious of them so they seemed more awkward than they actually were. But she was tall and graceful and, at times, her mother thought, as she watched her move silently and efficiently about her work, quite charming. Every time Big John went to town with the mail he marveled at the depth of the drifts, and compared this unprecedented fall with a "big snow" of twenty years before. The flakes never seemed to stop coming. Carried on the high, whirling winds they beat constantly in his face, no matter which direction he was going. As fast as the lake froze farther out it was massed deep with white. When he returned to the cabin at night he shoveled huge drifts from the door before he entered, and the floor boards near the threshold were constantly wet with snow which had seeped in through the cracks and melted there. As he threw shovelful after shovelful away from the path to the woodpile, he wondered at the relentlessness of the soft, inanimate stuff. If one were lost and helpless in the woods he would soon be covered, flake by flake, falling endlessly. All the trails were blocked and he had to use snowshoes constantly.

By the middle of December the snow was up to the roof-line of their cabin and still coming. Big drifts were piled by the unchecked winds sweeping across the lake and packed against the trees, higher than the house. Each day the windows were harder to clear, and the cabin became permanently as dusky as late twilight. The Indians did not mind, for the house was warm and they had all the fuel they needed, even for a longer, colder winter than they had expected. But the darkness and the constantly falling snow oppressed the Strange Woman. She could not leave the house unless on snowshoes, and they could not seem to teach her how to manage them. She paid no attention to Deneece and left her entirely to the care of Mrs. Big John and Kahnee. There were times when the Indians felt that she had no affection for the Child, for she never spoke to her, or tried to teach her to speak her own strange language.

Finally she performed only those tasks of the housekeeping which had been definitely assigned to her, and then sat, withdrawn from the family, staring intently through the window at the buried trail to the cabin as though now again she momentarily expected to see someone who never came. Occasionally her eyes would fix and remain set in a trance-like stare, and when the Big Johns saw her in this condition they knew she was striving to look back into her past. After a time she would shake her head hopelessly and drop again into that despondent attitude which had become habitual. When the windows were so thick with frost that there was no sight at all of the outdoors and the branches of the trees lashed savagely against the house, the old terror appeared in her eyes again and even in the safety of the cabin she glanced swiftly over her shoulder, afraid that the unseen Someone had entered and was staring at her there. She was quiet and patient, however, and the Big Johns became almost as fond of her as they were of the Child. And now they ceased to believe that sometime the Woman and Child might be taken from them by some person to whom they rightfully belonged. More than two years had elapsed and nothing had happened. Her attitude when she had first arrived with Big John had led them to hope she would in time be happy, but they knew now that they had been expecting the impossible. Music seemed to reassure her more quickly than words, and she was intently quiet when in the evenings Jane Big John cuddled the Child in her arms and rocked and sang her to sleep with the old tribal child-song of the White, or Naked Bear.

"Ka'ybo ma'wiken abijin'ojins,
Wabishki muk'wah kee gah tah'wahmig.
Kababishens! Kego goshkosikebinaguenigen."

"Do not cry, baby.
The white bear will bite you.
Screech owl!
Do not awaken him
By touching his head!"

As the old Indian droned the lovely, musical words over and over, the baby's eyes closed, the strange Woman lost momentarily her fear, and Kahnee and Big John seemed lost in reverie. And in this way the evenings passed.

On Christmas Eve a howling blizzard raged down upon them from the north and the Big Johns had to give up their idea of going to the Christmas Tree celebration in the schoolhouse, in the Settlement. Only those who lived close to the school could attend, and even they had to fight their way to the program and back again. But a few days after Christmas, when the gale had ceased and the snow had packed somewhat, the Big Johns heard a loud knocking at their door one night and opened it to admit Theophile Vargatte. He stamped the loose, clinging snow from his pacs and grinned cheerfully at all of them. Mrs. Big John greeted him more cordially than she did most whites for she always was delighted to see him. Now she inquired for Delima and if they had lately heard from Armand.

"Delima has been wondering how you were weathering this so-bad gale and liking this very-deep snow, so she insisted that I shall come over and find out for her," he answered as he pulled from his pockets the new pipe and the fine-cut tobacco which his wife had sent her. Then he pulled from an inner, protected pocket a small doll for the Child. "We were distressed that you could not come to the program for these were on the Tree for you, but when that great wind came upon us from the Canadian hills, I knew you could not come through it."

Then the men and Mrs. Big John drew out their pipes, filled and lighted them and sat companionably close to the hot stove for one of their long-deferred visits. Theophile told them all the news of the Settlement, what Armand wrote in his letters to them from Montreal, and also what he had gleaned from the newspapers. The Big Johns sat and listened to every word, showing their appreciation only by an odd grunt of agreement and approval uttered occasionally as he spoke of particularly interesting events. Even the Strange Woman worked up closer to the little group to hear what was said, and to feel that she belonged to the compact group. Theophile noticed her but did not speak, for Big John had told him she was once again easily frightened. Then, when all the news had been told on both sides, the Frenchman must see the Child. She was asleep in the small box-crib Big John had made for her, in one dim corner of the big living room. Mrs. Big John proudly held the lamp so its rays would not fall directly into the Child's eyes, and she did not waken. Theophile gazed at her in astonishment, for she was even more lovely than he had believed from Big John's descriptions. He had thought Big John was exaggerating, but as he looked down at her he wished with all his heart that he and Delima had a little girl as beautiful as this Child from nowhere. Her hair was silky, copper ringlets and her perfectly formed features and oval face were pink and white as the thornapple blossom in the Spring. He looked across at Big John and his eyes were so full of admiration that even the big Indian was satisfied. "Never have I seen so lovely a child," he commented. "She is as beautiful as a drop of clear water. I wish Delima could see her! Are her eyes also as beautiful?"

Big John was disturbed by the question though he could not understand why. "Yes," he answered slowly, using English for some obscure reason, "They are good eye and blue color like a flower. He is pretty baby and it is to us as if he belong now. We are goin' keep him both here long as we can. He will have to go his cabin sometime, mebbe, but we keep him till Jennie come home again. Then mebbe we don't have room no more, but we make a place till Jennie come."

Theophile laughed and there was affection in his eyes for Big John as he said, "I know you will make the room, Big John. It is only the way of you and you are always over-the-doing in good deeds. You and Mrs. Big John have made the room for many who needed help. And now I shall tell you what Delima has sent me here to tell. We wish your consent before we bare our plans to Abe. In the store he has worked hard since he came to stay with us, for it is the kind of work he likes to do. In many ways he is a wicked rascal, as we both have said before, Big John, many times. But also he has the good in him and this part of the boy comes out when he is with Delima. She is lonely, more than she will say, with our Armand gone so far away, and she wished me to say that we will keep Abe with us for as long time as he is contented to stay. We will send him to school and he can help in the store. As I have said, Big John, he has some very bad habits, and we may not change him greatly, but we will try. He cannot take the place of our Armand and we are not wishing that he shall, but we will be good to him. Mrs. Big John is better than she has been, and I am glad. So will be Delima when I tell her. But Mrs. Big John should not have such a one as Abe. She is too easy for him, for he is hard and not like her boys. If you agree, then we shall keep Abe, at any rate until the Strange Woman leaves your cabin. So we, too, shall have a share in this good-doing. Delima wants that Abe shall go to church also."

Big John smiled. "That is good. Abe like your place better as this one, and she will be good with you." Mrs. Big John nodded assent when he looked to her for approval. "Then that's settled," said Theophile and donned his mackinaw and snowshoes. He shook hands with them all and departed.

For a while they sat quietly after Theophile went. They liked to sit and ponder events silently and at leisure. Then Mrs. Big John said, and in her voice there was a wistfulness of which she was not aware, "So much of change has come to us this winter. Our boys are gone, doing now a man's work. Jennie and Waubegoon are not with us, yet it has not been long ago that they laughed together as they worked and played. The Child is here and the Strange Woman, no one knows how or why. And now goes the small bad Abe whom I could not touch with words or kindnesses. What more of change is to come!" Then Kahnee, the silent one, answered, and what she said startled them as though the big boulder on the beach had suddenly spoken. "One more change, my mother. When the big snow begins to melt, I shall marry with Moses Katemishkid. The missionary will come in March, and we shall marry in the church. I want a pretty dress to wear at my marriage." So, two months later, Big John bought at the store some white goods which Mrs. Vargatte said would be suitable, and the dress was made by one of the Settlement women. Kahnee went about deliberately as ever, and as silently, but her brown eyes were shining and she smiled constantly. Abe teased her and Moses every time he came home and found them both there, but they did not seem to hear or notice. The Missionary was delayed until the last week in April. The hard winter had retarded his work over the big territory which he served, and each small church had to wait its turn. But when he came they were wed in the church. The buds were already swelling on the maples, though much snow still lay in the woods and the trails were running deep with melted snow-water. The old oak tree at the bend in the trail had dropped the last withered leaf, and the cedars were newly fragrant. The Strange Woman would not accompany them to the church, but Big John took the Child, for he wanted Mrs. Vargatte to see and admire her. When they reached the church the Vargattes were there and most of the people in the Settlement. The old Missionary, frail, noble in feature, wise beyond all other white men in the ways and language of the Indians, took the two who were to be wed into the small room behind the altar and gave them wise advice. Then they came into the church and the marriage ceremony was performed. It seemed solemn and reverent, there in the little, snow-white church, so simply adorned with pictures and paper flowers. Even the Child sat quietly in Mrs. Big John's arms, entranced with the bright Spring sunlight streaming in long mote-filled shafts through the narrow windows. The beautiful Indian words with which the priest closed the ceremony were a fitting climax.

For the time, Moses and Kahnee were to live at the Big John cabin. It was the most satisfactory arrangement for all. So there was no rush of getting away on a wedding journey and they stood at the back of the church receiving the good wishes of their friends. Big John stood with them, but he was watching intently the women crowding around Mrs. Big John and the Child, with cries of curiosity and admiration. They cooed at Deneece, tried to talk with her, and attempted in every fashion to draw and hold her attention. She looked at them vaguely and smiled momentarily, then turned her head to the sunlight. Mrs. Vargatte took her from Mrs. Big John with little exclamations of delight at her beauty. Two other French women stood close, also admiring her. Then they began to ask questions. Had the Child made no attempt to talk? Had she not tried to say words? Not even the Indian words? Had she walked? Many other things they asked, then shook their heads and walked away. As Mrs. Vargatte kissed the Child's cheek and handed her tenderly to Mrs. Big John, the two other women passed close by Big John. He could not help hearing what one said to the other in a shocked voice, "I wonder if they do not yet know that that Child is not right!" And the other answered, "Hush. Mrs. Vargatte will tell them the Child is imbecile."

Big John had never heard the word. He strode over to Mrs. Vargatte. "Tell me, Madame Vargatte," he begged, "What means that word 'imbecile'?"

Delima Vargatte gasped. "And who has been so cruel as to use that so- horrible word!"

Big John insisted. "Tell me what they say, using that word."

Mrs. Vargatte gave in. It was better that they should hear it from one who would tell them kindly. It means, Monsieur Big John and Madame Big John, that the Child will never be like other children. It is a word we French people use to say that the brain is not right. The Child should now talk and walk, and she does not. Her eyes are too-empty. But do not worry about it now, for later we shall all see what can be done for her and she may get better as she grows."

She had expected sorrow from both her Indian friends at her explanation, and was astonished at Big John's sudden flashing smile of pure happiness. It was all beyond her comprehension. Still wondering at their response, she said her adieus and went home to Theophile with the sad news.

When the church was emptied of all but the Big Johns, waiting for the priest who was coming home with them to dinner as soon as he changed his robes, for he was a dear friend as well as priest to them, they looked at each other as though they had just heard a wonderful announcement. Big John could keep silence no longer. "Now indeed we do not need to worry, for luck will follow the tribe as long as it keeps the Child with it. The Child is ours, given freely by Manitou and twice-touched by him. The hair of red-copper and good luck, and the clean mind which shall hear only what Manitou wishes. The priest came to the door, ready to go with them. He, even with all his knowledge of his Indians, and because he was deep in reverie of what he hoped to accomplish before he was taken from them all, thought only that their unusual happiness and light-heartedness came because Kahnee had at last wed with the one she had planned for many years. To him, happiness in such a case was only natural.

CHAPTER VIII
WAUBEGOON PAYS THE FORFEIT

**SYMBOL OF POWER OVER
THE HEART OF A WOMAN**

WAUBEGOON PAYS THE FORFEIT

Almost before the Islanders realized that time was flying, May was half gone. Days were long again, the lake had opened, the first boat up the channel had been cheered, and bird calls were gay in the woods. When Big John came back from town one day with the mail, and, as usual, had waited until Mr. Vargatte had sorted and distributed the letters and had read his own, hoping for a quiet visit with his friend, Theophile grinned at him with great satisfaction. "Mon Dieu," he said gayly. "It is just as I thought would happen, me. Wait until I call Delima, and I shall tell you then what it reads in this letter from Telesphore."

Big John smiled in anticipation of what he was about to hear. Evidently Telesphore Dinet was coming to the Island again, just as he had promised. Delima came into the store, wiping her hands on a spotless towel, and sputtering with feigned impatience. "What he wants now, this so-crazee man! I must hurry and washing my dishes, and he brings me from my works to hear his letter from that so carefree Telesphore of ours!"

Both men laughed with her. "You will be surprised, then, when I read this letter, me!" taunted Theophile." Oh hurry, my Theophile," she coaxed. "What did Telesphore done now?"

So, without further foolishness, Mr. Vargatte read to his two intent listeners the startling news that Telesphore was returning to the Island, and his return would be a honeymoon trip. He had wooed and won Madeline, whether with tribal love-charms or not, he did not impart to them. The very next week they would arrive on the "Company" launch, which was stopping for two hours at their dock on its way down river, and there would pick up the dredge-men and hangers-on, and then go fifteen miles farther down the lake to the new location where they would be deepening the "Cut." He had written to the manager, who was a good friend of his, and had received permission to ride to Vargatte's dock, where the Island out-landers would embark. This he stated clearly and repeated several times, so his cousins would understand they did not have to meet him up at the town.

Delima turned to Big John. She was delighted with the news from Telesphore but was concerned at the way in which this letter would affect him. "Think you then that Waubegoon will go with Bill Crash and his wicked mother? They board the dredge men and will go with the workers. The chance has not come to me before now to 'tell you that Mrs. Crash has told all over the Island that Waubegoon's child has arrived."

Big John stared at her.

"True it is, my friend," corroborated Mr. Vargatte. "I had heard it last week, me, and I had thought that you already knew of it but were keeping silence. But of course she will go with Bill Crash," he informed Delima. "Why should she not go?"

"Her uncertain trail now goes farther from ours," said Big John, almost to himself.

"But no, Big John," hastily contradicted Theophile. "What then are fifteen miles! Will you anyway help us to plan a big reception for Telesphore and his bride? On a honeymoon the new-wedded ones must not step into sadness. We shall close the store for that afternoon and have a huge picnic in our grove, right close to the dock, and everyone must come. Immediately this minute then we must pass the words about, so his many friends will be here to greet him when he and Madeline first step from the boat. Come, Big John. Forget your trouble for a little time and help us to make merry."

Big John assented absent-mindedly and departed. After he had gone, Delima turned to her husband and held tightly to his hand" "Oh, Theophile! Trouble is coming again to our friend! As our Big John went out that door I heard the soft organ tone, clearer than any I have yet heard. I am shaking now with the echoes of it." Then she smiled up at him, though her eyes were misty with tears. "This is a great foolishness. What trouble could possibly come in company with his good friend Telesphore! Come then in to supper, and we shall plan the big picnic. I do not like to think that Monsieur Big John must tell the news to Madame Big John that Waubegoon leaves the Island.

"Your organ music is wrong this time," consoled her husband, "for Telesphore would never bring trouble to his friends."

However, Big John told Mrs. Big John only that Telesphore was coming, and of Vargatte's great plans for the wedding celebration. He did not tell her of Waubegoon. It was only one week longer that she would be on the Island, and chance might have it that she would go away with Bill Crash and his mother and Mrs. Big John would not know of it for a long time. If Waubegoon should choose to return to them, there was time enough for Jane Big John to be prepared for such happiness. Reticent Indian visitors would not be likely to give her such information, and she could not attend the picnic. He felt almost sure that this knowledge would not reach her until something definite occurred which would make it necessary to tell her.

So the week passed, with Big John and Kahnee guarding her from chance information about Waubegoon. On the day of the picnic he offered to remain with her quietly at home, but she positively refused to listen to him. She would be well enough with the Strange Woman and the Child for companions, she insisted, and she was expecting the Very Oldest Woman later in the afternoon to visit them. He was to take Kahnee and Moses and be there at the dock in time to greet his friend. At the last moment she put into their hands a gift for the bride, a birch cosso full of creamy sugar.

Elaborate preparations had been made at the Vargatte's grove, and already a crowd of old friends had gathered. Big John looked about at the familiar faces of the friendly Settlement people and was glad he lived among them. He spoke courteously to Mrs. Delongue and Mrs. Vargatte, and stopped a moment to listen to their exclamations of delight at the beautiful, sunny day, perfect for honey-mooners and a happy reunion of friends. Then he saw Sara, and Fred Mokok, and Kenebeg, and Fred had his great bow and many arrows in his hands. Big John moved closer to Sara, who sensed what he wished to ask. "Yes," she said, "we are to have many kinds of races and feats of skill. Some are to swim, some will wrestle, some will run with their feet tied together, and in other ways also. But Fred will shoot at that target on the big hemlock tree from many paces off. Kenebeg has challenged anyone to exhibit equal shooting skill.

Big John was reassured. He had kept so close to his own house that he had not known of the plans for the games. He wandered through the woods, looking for Waubegoon and Bill Crash, who were leaving on the boat which would bring Telesphore. Moses Katemishkid joined Fred and Kenebeg after his short-sighted, red eyes finally recognized them. Kahnee followed her father, knowing intuitively what he was seeking. And suddenly they came upon Waubegoon, alone, on the edge of the crowd. She was sitting on a fallen tree, her small feet buried deep in the plumy, silken moss under it, and she was holding a child in her arms. They had heard that she had named it Zshesheebans, the Little Duckling. Kahnee ached with the desire to touch the wee thing with her big, awkward hands. They could faintly hear the old lullaby she was crooning to it:

>"Little white nestling,
>Little white feather,
>Why dost thou not sleep--
>Here in this safe place,
>Here among beauty,
>Here must thou fear not
>So safe in my arms.
>Little white feather,
>Little white nestling."

    She was beautiful, sitting there, in her old fashion lost in dreams and in happy thoughts of her child. Her lips were curved in a gentle smile. Her soft hair was glossy black. The sun shone full upon her and brought out in the woods behind her the yellow gleam of cowslips. Big John wondered if she would ever lose that flower-like fragility of hers for which she had been named. They did not break her reverie, though they would have given much to know how she would have welcomed them. The overtures must now come from her; they could not thrust themselves upon her. They saw the Very Oldest Woman coming through the woods toward her, so they rejoined the group. Kahnee looked back longingly and noticed that the Very Oldest Mother had seated herself on the log beside Waubegoon, and they were obviously speaking of the baby. Then came a loud cry that the boat had tied up, and there was a general rush toward the land end of the dock. Big John, standing back a little, saw Bill Crash and his mother carried along unwillingly for a short distance, then pull themselves out of the pushing group and stand close to Fred and Kenebeg. He also noted that the arrows had been knocked from Fred's hands and trampled upon in the rush. He noticed that Waubegoon and the Very Oldest Woman were coming over to stand by Bill Crash, the Very Oldest Woman carrying the baby. Then he saw Telesphore and his bride, so close beside him that he could catch the gleam of his white teeth through his smile, and for the moment forgot everything else but his pleasure at seeing his friend and welcoming him.

And Telesphore saw no one in the crowd but Big John. His eyes flashed with pleasure, then misted with facile tears. Telesphore had a keen appreciation of the dramatic possibilities of any situation, and all unconsciously made the most of them, although he was capable of very real feeling. "Ah, mon vieux ami," he called across the short intervening space, until he could reach his friend. Then he threw his arms about Big John's neck and kissed him noisily on both cheeks, from sheer exuberance of joy. Telesphore's mother had been a pure-blood Ojibway Indian, but Telesphore followed the French customs of his father. Then he swung the big Indian around to face the eager-eyed girl who was staring at them. "This, then, is my old friend, Monsieur Big John," he introduced them, "and this is Madeline." Big John looked into the brown eyes twinkling up at him, at the tip-tilted corners of the sensitive, smiling mouth, and knew the girl was the one Telesphore should have. She spoke to him in French, as if she had always been one of the Islanders. "I have heard much of the family of Monsieur Big John. I am eager to meet Madame Big John. Is she well and is she here at our picnic?"

Telesphore laughed as gleefully as a child "Yes, Big John," he interposed, "Where is Madame Big John? We have brought for her that beautiful purple dress which we promised last winter. We had a gay afternoon choosing it, greatly daring, for we knew not the proper size." Big John's expression altered. "She is not well, and could not come to the celebration for your wedding. She sent this, however, as a small gift for the bride."

And then Madeline learned her first Indian word. Telesphore turned to her and said swiftly in undertones, "Say 'megwetch', Sweetheart. It means 'thank you' and will please Big John."

The Very Oldest Mother was not over-much concerned with Telesphore and his young bride. She had seen many youthful couples in her long years, and they were all quite alike. Vigilantly she watched her son, Kenebeg, talking seriously with Fred, and wished he would look at her and speak. Fred stooped to gather his arrows from the ground. At first he believed they were all shattered; then he saw that one was unbroken, the strong white-tipped arrow. He held it in his big fingers, looking at it dazedly. The Very Oldest Woman shifted her gaze from Kenebeg to Fred and shook her head mournfully. Then she muttered, so low that only Waubegoon heard and wondered, "Last night the spirit-light of Mujji-Muhnedo came silently from the swamp and circled stealthily around my cabin. I opened the door and in my mouth, under the tongue, I put the black earth, and some in each hand clenched tight, but evil that I could not see came with the light. Aih-ah! Evil is close this moment, yet I cannot see it--I cannot see it!"

Bill Crash grasped Waubegoon's arm roughly. "Don't listen to that damned old hag. Git the kid off her and come along. The boat's waitin'." You Injuns are a funny bunch. An old woman can whisper to you, and you git the jitters. Let's git outta here."

At that moment Fred Mokok stood up suddenly and decisively, as if a certain, heretofore undecided purpose had become motivated into definite action. "The white-tipped arrow," he said to Kenebeg, and his voice rasped in frenzy. "The white-tipped arrow! A sign! A sign! The aim must be sure and the speed swift. The forfeit of unfaithfulness must be paid."

They cautiously circled the group until they reached a point where Waubegoon was not between Fred and Bill Crash. The Very Oldest Woman watched speculatively, but being slow in movement and burdened with Waubegoon's child, she could not follow them. Then, too late, it came upon her what evil was about to happen. She could not prevent it unless she could call a warning in her shrill old voice above the gay laughter and talking of the crowd. Kenebeg heard her screaming, and knew the others would hear it in an instant. "May Mujji Muhnedo take that old fiend, my mother," he whispered. "Quick now, Fred! There is nothing between the Flower and you. You have a right to demand the forfeit!"

Fred looked at him strangely. "But my arrow is for him! She was but the blossom in his path that was trampled under his foul feet." Then he raised the bow and in an instant the string was taut and the white-tipped arrow was ready to fly to its mark, straight to the breast of Bill. A groan went up from the aghast group, aware now of what was happening but too far away to interfere. Bill, warned by the cry of the Very Oldest Woman, looked across at Fred Mokok, and the eyes of the two hating men met. In that glance two alien races stared at each other and gauged the wrong that each had done to each. Then Bill tossed his head and grinned at the inevitable, certain death that was coming toward him. Even in that taut moment these primitive spectators had a feeling of admiration for his unflinching, brash courage. Kenebeg's red tongue darted in and out, wetting his dry lips, and in the dead silence an evil hissing seemed to accompany the sound of the straining thong as Fred stretched it to release the arrow. Telesphore launched himself across the space separating them, but even as he began his rush, the arrow left the bow. Just as Fred's fingers released the arrow, Kenebeg reached out as swiftly as that striking snake for which he was named, and pulled Fred's arm. Beautifully straight and speedy the arrow flew to the direction Kenebeg planned. The force of the blow knocked Waubegoon to the ground, and the arrow pierced as deep as its barbs into her body, close to her heart. The crowd rushed toward her, but Telesphore was already kneeling there, raising her in gentle arms and shouting to the people to stand back. Mrs. Vargatte covered her eyes with her trembling hands so she could not see Waubegoon lying there at her feet. Fred stared at her as if he did not know what had happened. Then a terrible groan broke from his lips. He turned, and with a swiftness which matched Kenebeg's own, struck him with the heavy bow. Kenebeg fell and lay still. Women screamed. Children ran from their games and wedged themselves between their parents and stared with big eyes full of curiosity. Mrs. Delongue ran to the store for cloths which might be used for bandages. Some of the women sped to the beach to get water. Confusion was rampant, and any further untoward incident might turn it into a panic of revenge.

  At that moment the Very Oldest Woman stepped out from the others and came to Telesphore. She stood up straight and tall before them. She seemed aged yet ageless. Her face was rigidly stern and commanding. She had been transformed into a forbidding, meaningful and legendary figure. The group was silenced, and looked at her as if they had never rightly seen her before. It was as though the Black Shadow, personified, suddenly stood confronting them. She lifted one thin, blue-veined hand high above them. "Place her again on the grass, but ease her head from the ground's hardness," she commanded Telesphore, and like a child he obeyed. He looked up at her then, his brown eyes pleading with Fate itself. She answered his unspoken question. "I knew Evil was close, but could not foretell where it would strike. The Flower is dying. It is useless to try to pull out the arrow. The evil barbs will tear the flesh. Her life will come with it, and more pain is unnecessary."

Waubegoon opened her eyes. They were dim as if she were sleepy, then came awake with pain and surprise. She had heard what the Very Oldest Woman had said. She stared at her red-stained dress, and touched the wetness of it with her hand, as if she must assure herself of its reality. She looked up at the Very Oldest Woman, and the pathos in her eyes wrung Telesphore. "I am dying, Oldest one? Then the forfeit is paid, though I am young to die."

Big John bent close over her and she knew him. Her hand came up weakly and touched his cheek. "My father! The pain is great! Wait a little while with me. Aih-ah, I am tired, --and very cold---my eyes do not see you---"

She became quiet, and was so pallid they feared she was dead. Then again she roused and spoke wildly, frantically. "Talk to me, my father. I am afraid--to--go--alone--the dark-----talk-------"

Big John groaned. "Speak with her, Telesphore. I cannot. Speak you with her. She will not feel alone, so!"

So Telesphore spoke, but with a great effort, his cool palms caressing her forehead, "You are going away, 'tis true, Waubegoon, just as the Very Oldest Woman has said, but you will bloom again on the Happy Islands of our tribe. You will be warm there, Waubegoon, for the sun always shines, and Flowers that have been trampled and crushed in this world come into a fresh blossoming there. And you shall surely find light, and happiness, and love --and love too, Little Flower."

He could not force another word through his constricted throat, and bending carefully to avoid touching the arrow, he kissed her where her soft hair drifted back in a V from her forehead. Her eyes remained closed. He looked up at Big John. "She is dead!" he said and his voice was flat and toneless. "So quickly and without speaking to us again, she has died, our Little Flower!"

Big John stared at him helplessly. All his great strength seemed to have drained out of him leaving him sagging on his feet. As usual, his first thought was of his wife, and how he should tell her. Fred Mokok crept closer, but no one looked at him. The Very Oldest Woman grasped him by the arm. "Fred Mokok," she announced. "You will go to the town and give yourself up to white man's law. Indian codes gave you long ago the right to demand the life forfeit, but the law of this country says that shall be true no longer."

Fred gazed down, seeing nothing but Waubegoon. Finally he spoke, as though they two were alone. "This was not my wish, Little Flower. Believe me, it was not you I did desire to kill. But you are gone now, where neither revenge nor woe can follow. You are beyond all hurt and sorrow, and for that I am glad. I will give myself up to the law, for this was not my intent." He turned then, and went up toward the store. No one stopped him for they all knew he would do the thing he promised.

The Very Oldest Woman spoke to Big John. "You must not be so stunned by this thing which has happened. A Flower soon wilts, but always there comes another as fair and beautiful to take its place. Life goes on, for none is indispensable." She turned to Bill Crash, where he and his mother stood, overwhelmed and for once as silent as any Islander. Mrs. Crash had lost her truculence, and many wondered what thoughts of the Flower were passing through her mind, and if regret were there also. The Very Oldest Woman counseled both of them. "Go now, as you had planned. Take the baby, for the Flower would wish you to have it. Life is at fault, not you. Life trends downward through deep-forested valleys. Each must follow his own trail alone to the end whether he go willingly or no. The Wise Ones say the Trail leads to happiness, but who has ever retraced his steps to tell what lies beyond the End. We are bewildered by the shadows cast around us to limit our vision. And always the Black Shadow follows close behind us. Those we are to meet or pass on the Trail may not be avoided. Some are easily wearied. Some are too hurt by life, like the Flower, and for them the Path is mercifully shortened, but for others of us --for others of us-"

She faltered as if she were too weary to stand, appeared to shrink in size, and now the illusion that had held them all speechless while she held command over them, faded, and she was nothing but their own Very Oldest Woman, who was most humanly frail and weak. Telesphore put his arms close about her so she would not fail. "You are brave and wonderful, Very Oldest One," he commended. "Now sit you there and let me take charge of this thing." He, too, turned to Bill. "Do as the Oldest Mother has advised," he ordered. "Later, when we shall need you at what must follow in law, we shall know where to find you. The boat goes in a minute. Board it, else no one knows what may yet happen here. Leave Waubegoon here with her own people. Madeline, will you take Madame Vargatte to the house? We must all go and leave Big John and Kahnee alone with Waubegoon and their great grief. But yes, and Theophile and I must go to town for the doctor, and the Flower must not be moved from this place. Leave her quietly there among the broken blue violets until we shall return. That is the law!"

Slowly the crowd dispersed at his suggestion, knowing he was right, respecting him and muttering their sympathy to Big John as they passed, until there was left only Big John, Kahnee and the Very Oldest Woman. After a long time Big John asked Kahnee if she would wait there until he could go home to prepare Mrs. Big John for what was to come. He would return to her as quickly as he could. She nodded. He asked Moses to go with him and remain with Mrs. Big John, and they disappeared down the trail.

The slumbrous dusk was falling in the grove. Tall trees stretched their shadows farther from the sun as they waited for the night. The sounds of the departing boats came over the water and echoed from the hills; the slow, steady hum of the work-boat sounding like an undertone to the staccato popping of the speed-boat engine of Mr. Vargatte's racer as it hurried to town. Birds twittered cheerfully among the branches overhead as they sought their nests. Kahnee sat by her young sister, and smoothed the tumbled hair from her forehead. She was pondering the truth of the words of the Very Oldest Woman. "Life goes on. No one is indispensable!" In the woods, life was already going on as though no tragedy had been enacted there. And she questioned where that spirit that had been Waubegoon had gone. A white-throat fluted somewhere in the distance, a long, sweet call. She shivered. That flute-note always seemed to come to her at some supreme moment of gladness or hurt or peace. Then she quieted and began to sing the old chant for the young dead. Her soft, monotonous little tune blended with the descending night and the drowsy bird-notes:

> "When you are told that I am gone,
> You will know where I am.
> My journey will be to that Island
> Far out in the lake.
> From that mirage-island
> No one has ever returned,
> And there I shall be lonesome
> Until you come----"

The Very Oldest Woman was haggardly weary, but she dragged herself over to Kenebeg, where he was still lying, part of a black shadow. "Go far away, my son, while the opportunity is still yours," she said tiredly. "You were placed upon an evil Trail when you were born, but you have walked it too gladly." He struggled to his feet and, weaving dizzily down the trail, merged with the bosky night gloom. When she could see him no longer, the Very Oldest Mother returned to Kahnee and sat close to her. She was indeed old and tired, and she would never see her ostracized son again. Black night was near, and she was glad Kahnee, the ever-dependable, was with her. She had never known fear, but times came when one needed another human close. Such need was hers now. She filled her worn pipe with tobacco from a flimsy white sack, and as she sat on the earth beside Kahnee and Waubegoon, listened dispassionately to the ancient lament for the young dead while she smoked.

> "Where I shall wait with longing.
> Even though I have my heart's desire.
> Until you come.
> Until you come!"

CHAPTER IX
MADELINE

**SYMBOL REPRESENTATIVE
OF WOMANHOOD**

MADELINE

Jennie came home in June. They were expecting almost any day to have her letter telling them to meet her in the town. A strange boat stopped at their dock one afternoon and three persons climbed out and came up the path to the cabin. When they were close enough to be recognized, Big John hastened to meet them. Jennie had returned, bringing with her two white people and he must make them welcome. Even in his side-long first glance at her before their greeting, Big John could see there had been a decided change in the girl, but he did not have a moment to analyze what that change might be, for Jennie immediately introduced her new friends to him. They were Mr. and Mrs. Brand, the superintendent of the Indian School, and his wife. Big John felt an instant liking for both. As they walked toward the house, Mr. Brand explained that he had business through the entire Upper Peninsula, so they had decided to bring Jennie home and at the same time see what the conditions were on the Island and if more Indian children could be persuaded to attend the Indian School. He was a quiet, unfluent man, friendly without being familiar, and had such a complete understanding of their situation that Big John found himself talking almost as freely with this stranger as he would with his close friend, Mr. Vargatte. Mrs. Brand was a straight-walking, reserved woman, but her smile was quick and friendly.

For an hour or longer, the school man asked pertinent questions and Big John answered them frankly. They discussed the land problem as it would affect Jennie and Joe Pete when they returned to the Island permanently, and they tentatively decided that the boy should go on to a more advanced school in another state, when he had learned the subjects taught at the Michigan Indian School. Mr. Brand explained to Big John how the school was conducted and what they hoped to accomplish with the Indian children there. He urged Big John to come to the school and see things for himself. Then he asked about the location of another Indian home he wished to visit, said goodbye, and departed immediately. Big John felt sorry to see him go. He had at last found a white man who did not repeat his farewells.

After the superintendent and his wife had gone, Kahnee and Jennie unpacked her clothes and the girl settled down again in the family routine as if she had never been away from it. However, to her mother's astonishment, she positively refused to help with the basket weaving, saying she had forgotten how, and there was a certain hard aloofness about her which they could not fathom or break through. Despite this, they were rejoiced to have her with them again. In answer to their questions she replied quietly that she liked the school and people were all good to her there. She described the buildings, outlined the schedule, and characterized some of the teachers, but impassively and with none of her old impishness. Joe Pete was well and was quickly learning everything Mr. Brand had suggested to him. There was an ironic note in her voice when she mentioned Joe Pete's name which puzzled them, but they did not press her to explain. When Kahnee asked her to accompany them on their customary check-up trip over to the unused hunting lodge which Jerry had left in trust for Joe Pete, she would not go. The day was too warm, she said evasively, and they must realize that no one would break into a log shanty anyway. There was nothing in it that anyone would want to carry off. Kahnee stared at her in astonishment and answered that if she and Moses had a cabin as good and as comfortably furnished as this which Jennie refused to become excited about, they would feel they had everything one could ever desire from life. Jennie laughed mirthlessly and would not discuss the matter. Even though her laughter was forced at times, they enjoyed hearing her voice in a house which had been too-long empty of it, so they teased her about her now-scrupulous cleanliness and fear of germs, and her new fashioned ways of cooking their usual food. In spite of her nasty little attitude of superiority over them, her grace and charm cheered Mrs. Big John more than she would admit, even to herself. There was a delicate frangibility of bloom upon the girl and she was wistfully beautiful. She was slender and moved with a swaying grace and ease which made her mother think of elfin silver poplars shaking out their drapery of glistening leaves against rose-tinted, Spring-morning skies. Kahnee admired her whole-heartedly and without envy, and felt that, in her own way, Jennie was more lovely than Waubegoon had been. They decided to enjoy the few months she would be home. Too soon she would leave them again, for she was determined to return to the Indian School as soon as it opened in September.

Between Madeline, Telesphore's winsome bride, and Jennie there grew a sincere admiration which soon became close friendship. Jennie respected and was somewhat awed by Madeline because she had always lived in a large city, which for Jennie would be the quintessence of pleasure. To Madeline, Jennie's nature-knowledge and her unIndianlike willingness to impart it to another were never-ceasing wonders. They were opposite in appearance and temperament, but each had much to give the other. The Big John baskets delighted Madeline with their color and shape and their elusive yet lingering odor of sweet-grass. Mrs. Big John always smiled when the city girl held the fragrant things close to her nose and remarked that the perfume of the grass would always bring the Island back to her in memory, no matter where she might be. She bought every lovely one she could afford and sent them to her friends. Before long it became an accepted custom that Madeline would wander over to the Big John cabin in the afternoon, and when the store was closed for the day, Telesphore, and occasionally Theophile and Delima also, would join her there for a leisurely stroll home through the woods at dusk and their late supper. The bond between the two families seemed stronger than ever before. Sometimes Jennie met Madeline half-way on the trail and led her through dim, unexplored paths into moss-carpeted forest ravines and small, fern-fragrant clearings, where redstarts spread their gay orange feathers for their own secret admiration, hermit thrushes poured nostalgic, liquid music into the deep woods-silence, and the queer, dark-red crossbills flew in erratic circles among the pines and cedars.

One golden day they happened by chance on a tote-road which led them into a slashing, where years before there had been a lumber camp. The old buildings, made of the worthless poplar logs, stood sleepily in the sun like tired old gray ghosts, caught disheveled and off-guard in daylight. A rank growth of jewel-weed covered the ground and obliterated the once-used paths and even the trail. Coming from shadow into the sun-washed clearing, the girls stood a moment at the wood's edge, accustoming their light-blinded eyes to the glare. As they stood there, they were suddenly aware that the air above the jewel-weed was alive with bits of flashing, flying color. Warily they crept to the middle of the clearing and sat upon a huge stump there. But they might as well have come noisily, for those mites of living, burnished-metal brilliance were entirely unmindful of their presence. Hundreds of tiny birds darted to and fro among the jewel-weed and seemed to hang on velocity-blurred wings as they sipped the nectar in the dainty, orange cornucopias suspended from the tall stalks. In swift search they went from flower to flower, endlessly and beautifully, their green feathers and red throats gleaming and shimmering in the sunlight. Madeline sat so motionless as she ecstatically watched, that one lighted a moment upon her shoulder. When it flew again she felt on her cheek the tiny air currents from its fanning wings. "Oh the small beauties, What are they?" she whispered to Jennie.

"Do you really not know, then?" Jennie countered. But she smiled and her eyes became impish. "They are called nahno'-okkahse'eusug in the Indian."

"I cannot say that word." Madeline mourned, "and it is too long a word for such a wee fairy thing. Do you know the English name?"

Jennie nodded. "Mrs. Vargatte told me long ago that they were humming birds. They are nice, I suppose, but I would rather see town sights."

But after that day Jennie showed the city girl all the secret places of the Island woods and trails, which only the Indians knew. To Madeline the unspoiled, natural wildness; the blue-green of the crystal river which occasionally widened into lakes of far horizons; the meandering trails, going nowhere in particular; the huge, whispering black-green hemlocks and pines; the strange fragrance of shrubs and flowers; the little tree-sheltered cove in which Big John's cabin squatted close to the shore; all had the glamor of those dreams of beauty she had long imagined from Telesphore's descriptions in his letters to her, and which had now become actuality. For her, every common event had a dramatic quality out of all proportion to its casualness and naturalness. Because of this, Telesphore was delighted that she was at the Big Johns when the boys arrived from the wood camp.

The day had been warm and they had all wandered over to the dock, where the air seemed cooler. As the sun slipped down behind the mainland across the lake, the after-glow of orange-lavender and copper was intensified and heightened in the silk-smooth water. One red star hung so low on the horizon it seemed to be within arm's reach. A black freighter glided along out in the channel and after a time the waves from its noiseless passage washed great splashes of opal and amethyst against the piles below their feet. A blue heron, with long legs stretched straight out behind it, flapped clumsily to its shelter behind the Point. Shrilly-calling terns flirted with their reflections in darting swoops to the water. The white-throat fluted its music in the darkening woods and the veeries sang in the shadows. Madeline reached for and held Telesphore's hand, and there, before them all, he bent and kissed her clinging fingers.

"What does it all make you think of?" she asked him softly, disliking to break the velvety silence, but wanting to know what he drew there beside her. Telesphore shook his head, wishing to draw her out before the Big Johns that they might understand her better and like her greatly, as she deserved. "It is like a stage setting for a wonderful play," she continued, almost under her breath. "It is too enchanting to be real. Look at the old sandpiper, coaxing her spoiled babies along the shore to their hiding place. And see the mother duck out there in the reeds with her young ones trained like soldiers to obey instantly. And just back there in the woods, Telesphore, where the three brown trails meet among the spruces, is a place of such loveliness that I must always pause long enough to let the fairies step off the scene before I enter. Always when I have passed through, I look back to see if my passing is not the cue for their performance. Some day, when I belong here, like you and the Big Johns, and have the right, I shall not hesitate, and shall surprise those tiny winged ones playing their woods drama. I shall watch it to the end, Dearest, and then I shall write the most charming fairy story that ever has been written."

Telesphore laughed out joyously, and the Big Johns smiled. Then he said to her quickly, "And now your stage comes to life, my Sweet. Two players enter, exactly as if your words were a cue which has conjured them out of the night. Look! Coming around the Point there! It is indeed beautiful, as you have said."

Against the glowing sky was outlined the clean-cut shape of a canoe, and two men paddling rhythmically and without effort. Intently they watched it coming closer. Then Big John called, "It is the Magic Feather! Jim and our Young John are in it." The echoes of his voice came back faintly from the hills and the still woods, and

Jim raised his paddle high in salute while silver drops sparkled from its blade. They hurried to the end of the dock to welcome their boys.

As they all walked toward the house, Telesphore and Madeline suggested that they should go home, but their hosts would not listen. Jim offered to take them in the Magic Feather as far as Vargatte's dock, if they would promise to remain for the evening. Madeline was so eager to ride in the canoe that Telesphore laughed and agreed to stay.

Then at the cabin there was much talking, and quick laughter, and quiet moments of sorrow at the remembrance of Waubegoon's death, as they told each other all that had happened since they had last met. They spoke with commiseration of Fred Mokok's sentence of life imprisonment, as if it were not their sister he had killed. Madeline was beginning to understand their philosophy now, and did not wonder that they should have no resentment toward Fred. They tried courteously to include the Strange Woman in their conversation, but she was still shut away from them by the barrier of language which she could not break through, except with Telesphore. She saw only the Vargattes, Telesphore and the Indians, and occasionally the Jesuit missionary. The Indians used the Ojibway unless they were compelled to speak French or English out of courtesy to guests or in doing business with the whites. The Vargattes spoke always in French, and only when necessary dropped into the English or the Indian. Telesphore used all three, and more, as did the Missionary, without consciously knowing which he was speaking. Thus the Strange Woman constantly heard three languages, and the few words she mastered to express her wants were a conglomeration of all she heard spoken. The boys and Big John now planned to settle her once more in her own cabin, for with the boys home again the Big John house was full and she would be more comfortable alone. They exclaimed over the growth of the Child, and wondered a little why she did not attempt to talk. She was four years old, they figured, and Indian children were speaking long before they became that age. They wondered, but it was casual, for, after all, talking did not matter. She was beautiful, she had red hair, and she belonged to them.

After the first rush of talk and planning was over, Jim told his news. He and Young John, he admitted, had not come directly from the camps. They had been up at the town for a week, and Jim had purchased a certain thing there which would surprise them all.

He told them the article was too enormous to bring to the Island in a canoe, and had been left in a building on the mainland, which a farmer he knew had allowed him to use. He gave them each three guesses. Big John guessed that it was a new cow; Jennie hoped it was an organ; Kahnee and her mother smiled and did not offer an opinion. Telesphore laughingly hazarded an idea that it might be a car and was as amazed and excited as any of the others when Jim nodded his head. Jim had been doubtful as to what Big John might say about such an extravagance, but Young John could keep still no longer.

"It is one beautiful car, my father, and when you see it you will not say it was a foolish thing to buy. It is not like our old launch, bucking so frequently that we often must row to town if we wish to be sure of the mail. The county road on the Island is good enough for a car to travel, so now we shall ride to the head of the Island and row only across the Narrows to the town. We have already spoken to Mr. Lute, and tomorrow he brings the car across the lake on his scow, towed by the big Flambeau." He looked at his father anxiously, saw him smiling, and continued quickly. "For two days we looked at many kinds of cars, and rode in them all until our heads whirled. We were cautious and did not buy the first one we saw. Six men were trying all at one time to sell to us, though we were buying only one car. It was funny, my father. And this car Jim bought was only one year old and was of all those cars the best."

"What kind is it?" questioned Telesphore laughing delightedly at Young John's loquacity, and his white teeth flashed in the lamplight. "And why then did you not come and get me to assist you in such a big purchase?"

Jim grinned at him. "We did not want anyone to know of it. It is a red car, but that seller-man called it 'maroon', I believe."

"I mean, what is the name of the car? Who made it? Monsieur Henry Ford?" Telesphore was interested and amused. "The name of one man is not on the car," Jim explained. "It is named a Chevrolet. The man who owned it was a fine driver and the car has had good care. In the week the seller-man taught me to drive it, and he has already sent for my license. The car will seat five, so tomorrow we shall all drive to the Settlement in it."

Telesphore assured Big John several times that the boys had bought the car at a real bargain, and at last he was satisfied, though one hundred dollars seemed a great amount. It would be the first car on the Island, and the boys were appreciative of the excited comments it would cause. They talked until late, and Telesphore finally said they must go home. Jennie accompanied them to the end of the dock. She was walking close to Madeline, and putting an arm around her drew her a little apart from the others. "I am glad my brothers bought this car," she confided to Madeline. "I shall have them teach me to drive it. It will be something different to do, for I have lost entirely my taste for this place. I will not be a basket-weaving squaw, and I am not happy here where is nothing I wish to do. I shall be glad to go back again to the School, where there is pleasant work, and people, and fun, and shows sometimes. I hate this small cabin in which we all must live and crowd upon one another's feet. Since I have seen something better I carry a great discontent with me here."

Madeline hugged her. "Oh Jennie," she said softly, "you are so pretty and you belong with the enchantment of this place. Don't let yourself feel so discontented. We can't always do exactly as we wish, and we must think sometimes of others. Do you realize what you can do for the other Indian girls who have not had your chance?"

Jennie shrugged away from the embrace. The hard note had returned to her voice when she answered, slowly and deliberately. "You talk just like ---just like---" She hesitated, then went on bruskly, "Just like everybody else. What do I care for those other girls? I care only what happens to me! Why should I waste myself on them! They will not change, no matter what white people at the school may believe about it. They will cling to the old ways of shiftlessness. Let those who wish come back and teach them again the old crafts. Imagine an Indian being taught his own, old crafts by a white who thinks he knows better than the Indian what that craft is. I have decided that I shall not do it. I want a good time, me, and I intend to have it. And what is there for a woman on this Island but hard work and early old age?"

"But it is so lovely and unspoiled here, Jennie. Can't you believe that and be contented here again?"

"That is very well for you," Jennie answered with bitterness in her shrewish voice. "You will be going away before the bitter cold and loneliness come upon us here on the Island. Then what is left? Even your Telesphore had to run from it last winter. Here there is not one book to read, and their talk is ever of basket-trading, and boats to be made, and basket trading, and more boats, and more basket trading! And what have we to work with? Where shall we get things as the whites have? We come back to these old ones with our minds filled with new ways and our hearts eager to help, and they sit as fixed in their places and old customs as those old gray stones in our field. They will not change or let us follow the new ways they send us away to learn. I am weary of it, me, and happiness is not here now for me."

"Kahnee is content," Madeline tried to argue, though she was lost in the uselessness of it.

"Kahnee is the old Indian itself. She is more Indian than any of us, though we all are of straight Indian blood. She knows nothing better, and she is married with one she likes even though he is stupid and awkward. Have you never noticed how she sits! More silent than any. You will leave the Island and go to fun, and a nice place to live with those furnaces to keep you warm even without any work of putting in wood and coal. Telesphore is good to you beyond anything an Indian woman knows, even from the best Indian man on the Island. You will go to shows, and parties, and hear music. Would you change places with me? You see only the beauty, but I know the ugliness of the other side." Jennie spoke with such passionate fury that Madeline felt repulsed.

"But you are to marry Joe Pete, Jennie. You will never be like the others you speak of."

Jennie was about to respond, then as if she realized the hopelessness of making the other girl understand as she did, set her lips tightly and closed her eyes.

Madeline had to get into the canoe and go without saying more, for the men were waiting for her. "Goodnight, dear," she called as Jennie and Big John walked back to the house and the canoe glided out into the lake.

"Tomorrow I shall see you again, me," Jennie called after her, and because her father was listening she forced her voice to become natural again.

All the way up to Vargatte's store Telesphore and Jim laughed and talked. Madeline answered their questions and joined occasionally in the conversation, but she was wondering about Jennie and quite forgetting that she was at last riding in the Magic Feather. Big John had somehow looked older and more tired this night than she had ever seen him. She knew he was silently planning great things for the future when Jennie and Joe Pete should come home permanently. They were to lead the younger generation to better ways of living. But was Jennie never coming to stay? Was something wrong with Jennie and Joe Pete which Jennie was hiding under this bitter way of speaking? Would they never marry? She almost wept, for she felt that Big John's heart would break!

When Telesphore took her arm to guide her up the path to the store she dismissed Jennie and her problems from her mind. "They say each must walk his own trail," she thought. In the darkness she stumbled, and Telesphore clasped her close and kissed her. "Sweetheart," he whispered to her and she smiled. "Yes," she decided quickly. "The Indians are right and each has to walk his own trail. Jennie, Delima, Armand, Big John. Everybody!" In spite of her worry for the happiness of Big John and his family, she was suddenly filled with gladness that she was to walk her trail with Telesphore always close by.

CHAPTER X
CELESTINA

SYMBOL OF SOCIABILITY

CELESTINA

The end of September was close. Great, roaring winds that stretched their mighty wings high into the air swept the leaves in multi-colored clouds from the trees and scurried them dizzily in circles which leapt aloft and died down again, like scarlet and orange fires in the woods. Huge waves of dull gray battered at the Big John dock with the thicker, heavier sound of Autumn water. Small birds which still remained, sought the shelter of the deeper, greener woods, but the unabashed and jaunty blue-jays drifted in cerulean splashes across the meadows and trails and woods-clearings, calling their secret signals of migration to each other as they flew. Gold-and-white flickers hunched through the air as if they were rowing, with a perceptible slackening of speed between strokes. Meadowlarks sat dumpily on the fence posts, waiting for their call to fly southward. Sudden squalls dropped their curtain of rain, shrouding the cabin and obliterating horizons. Against this changing background floated the leaves, stem-first, and yet myriads clung stubbornly to the branches. All day and night they continuously scratched down across the roof of the Big John cabin, imitating the field-mice, Kahnee thought with irritation, as she sat weaving, close to the west window where the light was best during the shortening days. And just as she hated the blooming of the first golden-rod because of the queer, lonely feeling she experienced at the sight of it, so she particularly detested the chuckling jays when they gathered in flocks to leave the Island, for she knew winter followed close behind their flight. Now she was beginning to loathe the sight and sound of the falling, whirling, scraping leaves. The rain had kept her too long indoors, and no guests, not even Madeline, had come to the house. If she had been a white woman she would have found relief in a fit of temper, or in pacing the floor, but because she was Kahnee, and more an Indian than her uncivilized great-grandmother, for all her perturbation she sat stolidly at her task, meticulously sorting and matching her colors and never stopping even to look at the jays as they dropped impudently past her window. She had discovered when she was a very small child that there was futility in fretting about anything as inevitable as the changing seasons.

Though she lacked the comeliness of her two younger sisters, and was sensitively aware of it, Kahnee craved comrades, but had trained herself to watch quietly as her friends continually became attracted to more beautiful and accomplished persons and forgot her entirely, unless they wished a favor of her. Madeline liked her but could never break through her shell of aloofness. Mrs. Vargatte had sensed the girl's longing, and, because she was naturally sympathetic, had learned to appreciate her splendid qualities and finally had grown to love her more than she did the other two girls.

So Kahnee felt more at ease with the French woman than she did with her own people, for with her she could speak frankly of anything which came into her mind, and be sure of being understood. Even with Mrs. Vargatte she could not use those meaningless terms of endearment, the "dears and "darlings" which came so easily to Jennie and Waubegoon, who had them from the French girls in the Settlement. She had been an untouchable child, who loved too deeply and hated as bitterly, but this she kept secret and her own family was not cognizant of any variation in her attitudes. She never forgave or forgot a hurt, though she could make no outcry when she was wounded and even loved the person who had caused the pain. After a time she built a wall of icy reserve against further hurting from the intrusion of others into her life, and stoically accepted the knowledge that for her there would probably never be bosom friends or affection from other women. There was no bitterness in her, but her early awareness of the fact that people were not attracted to her, no matter how sincerely she might try to win them, caused her to draw within herself and at last cease making overtures. So, with the exception of Jim, who understood her better than did the others, it became a fixed idea with her family and sisters that she was insensitive and wooden, and she continued to love them undemonstratively but with fierce loyalty, and all unenviously missed them when they went away from the cabin. She had adored Waubegoon because of her frail beauty, but after Waubegoon had gone she had put Jennie in her place in her affections, though she was fully aware that Jennie despised her and thought her dull and uninteresting. When she was weary or ill, there were times even now, that she longed for a more understanding companionship than that which Moses, the Sluggard, was capable of offering her. Now she had a presentiment that Jennie had left them, somehow, and it was not of her physical absence that she was thinking.

Her unusual mood of introspection was broken by the sound of Jim's car pounding down the trail to the house. He had driven Jennie back to the Indian School, for they had discovered that it was quite easy to ferry the car across the Narrows on the big scow. To the Big Johns the Indian School seemed very far away, and it was an adventure for Jim to drive such a distance. He had promised to return speedily, yet he had been three weeks gone on the trip. Some irritation that had been pricking Kahnee's mind into uncommon rebellion ceased when she heard her brother's car approaching. There was a closer bond between them than they realized, and Jim always agreed with Kahnee against the others. She rose, and her mother and Big John looked up and smiled after her as she went to the door hurriedly to welcome Jim.

The car stopped at the gate and Jim opened its door. Then he turned to help someone else out. Kahnee stared. A short, plump girl grasped Jim's hand, climbed down and came up the path with him. Kahnee returned swiftly to the living room. This was a thing which her father and mother should know immediately. She spoke rapidly, to warn them. "Jim brings one with him. A girl! A stranger!"

Big John strode to the door, that a guest of a member of his family might not enter unwelcomed. Mrs. Big John rose and stood unsteadily, holding to the side of her rocker. Kahnee knew a sudden concern about this increasing weakness of her mother, and an amazed perception that her hair had become white during the last two years, and she was an old woman. Then the door opened and Jim and the girl came into the room. A mist from out-doors seemed to enter with them, and a yellow leaf scurried across the floor and stopped near Mrs. Big John's feet. For a moment no one spoke. Jim had not the gift of swift words, and the others waited for him to speak, as was courteous. They looked furtively at the girl as they waited. She was a childish thing, and reminded them of Waubegoon, but she was not like the Ojibway women. She was a round, softly curved girl, and though her skin was smooth as a flower petal, it was darker in pigment than theirs, and without the healthy reddish gleam which at times made their skins almost coppery colored. Her lips were fuller and more sensuous than Waubegoon's but beautifully shaped and firm. Her eyes puzzled them. They were huge in her face, which was shaped like the leaf of a violet, Kahnee thought wonderingly; and as nearly black as eyes can be, but the whites were so clear that they flashed as she looked patiently and with ill-concealed curiosity from Big John to the mother and then at Kahnee. Jim had obviously coached her as to her behavior and she was waiting judgment of her.

At last Big John found that he could speak in English, so the girl could understand. Jim said, "This is Celestina, my father, my mother, and Kahnee, my sister. He is now my wife, so I have brought him home with me."

Though they were astonished almost beyond belief or speech by the unexpectedness of the announcement, Big John remembered the courtesy due to a guest and his son's wife. He held out his hand to the girl, just as Mr. Vargatte would have done. "We are glad you have come, us," he greeted her gravely. Her eyes filled with tears but her mouth smiled gallantly. She held the big hand offered to her against her breast. "I am happy to see my new father," she answered gladly, and her voice held a sincerity which won Big John to her. Seeing this, Jim grinned with relief. If his father liked her, all was well. Then Kahnee came forward, for Mrs. Big John stood helpless and trembling beside her chair as if growing fast there. Kahnee also held out her hand, but Celestina stood on tip-toe, impulsively threw her arms tightly around Kahnee's neck and, to her astonishment, kissed her. That spontaneous kiss broke through Kahnee's exterior reserve, and in spite of herself she responded and clasped the newcomer close in her arms as something hard and icy melted within her to give place to a curious happiness. Again Celestina kissed her, and her lips were smooth and soft like those of a child against her own. "Do care for me a little bit, Ka-ah-nee," she pleaded like a small sister, and Kahnee had to smile. That smile was the one beautiful thing about Kahnee. "Already I like you, me," she said, and was surprised at her own words, for they were true. Jim stared as if he could not believe Kahnee had spoken.

Jim led the girl then to his mother. "Mother," he pleaded solemnly, "Do not be disappoint about this one I have married with. He is Indian, though not of our tribe. He is a Mexican girl." Mrs. Big John looked searchingly into the black eyes which stared questioningly into hers. Then Celestina saw the weakness of the old woman, and putting her strong young arms about her unhesitatingly, eased her again into the rocker. Mrs. Big John reached for Celestina's hand, and the girl bent and kissed the shrunken cheeks of her new mother. She made a valiant attempt to recover from an almost unbearable feeling of strangeness which threatened to overwhelm her and start a flood of tears. "Will you also like me just a little until I know you better?" she coaxed, and Mrs. Big John nodded. Celestina sped back to Kahnee as to an old friend, and Kahnee wondered gladly if the companionship she had craved had come with this girl. "Oh. Ka-ah-nee," she laughed. "I am so glad we are here at last, and your people like me; and they do, for Father Big John would not say so unless he spoke the truth." Then they all laughed and the tension was eased. They knew now that she was full of gay talk and thinking, like Telesphore. The house would never be silent and empty again as long as this merry child was in it. She continued, talking to Jim but including them all and they admired her bravery, for they understood that she was talking against a feeling of strangeness and insecurity and, probably, even great loneliness. Thus Waubegoon might have talked in the house of the Outlander's mother. They listened with grave attention to her chatter. "This house is so big and nice and it smells good, like a woods, but I think maybe it is from that grass which you have hanging on the wall there. It makes me think of a man I saw once at a Fair, who could make his voice seem to come from any place. That grass has his power, for it can make its fragrance come from other places than where it is. He was a ventriloquist, so that must be ventriloquist grass, Jim?"

    He nodded assent and she continued, talking through an ache in her throat. "My home, even since I came from Mexico, has always been a little sugar-beet cabin. Two or three rooms, and all of them might be placed in this one room. And I love the beautiful baskets you are making, and you will learn me to make them, too. And Jim says that never again will I have to work out in the beet fields, topping beets until my arms and shoulders ache so I cannot sleep at night. Jim, it is too good to be true, and ----"

    Jim interrupted with an apology. "Let me then tell my father and mother and sister about how I met you and what happened after. Do not care if I speak the Indian, for my mother does not understand good the English."

    "That is fair," she agreed and went over to sit by Kahnee.

So Jim the slow-speaking one, was forced to make the longest speech of his life, and he did it well, with an unsuspected touch of the Indian oratory. He told of the flat, monotonous country in the southern part of the state and the big, prosperous farms there, where great fields of sugar beets grew. He described vividly the Mexicans working in the fields; their wide, sometimes bell-trimmed hats; Celestina's short, swarthy father and mother with their sun-reddened eyes, and their long days of labor among the beets. He had to tell all the minute details that Big John might comprehend a thing so foreign to anything he had seen. He described the way he had leaned upon the fence and watched Celestina working in the field. She had smiled at him and he had spoken to her. Then they had met after her work was done and had sat on the steps of her little shanty home and talked. Finally they had decided to marry, and her parents had consented. As he pictured the frugal wedding meal, and the picturesque group of Mexicans sending them on their way, Big John ran his hands through his hair, in his old awkward gesture, setting it all endwise. For the first time it was made clear to him, through contact by one of his own family with another section of the country, and his vivid explanation of it, that other races than the Indians had troubles and problems which seemed to have no solution. He looked at Celestina with growing respect and sympathy, and when Jim's story was finished he had accepted her as one of their family and race.

Then Jim turned to Celestina. "Tell them then about you, more than I can tell them, for it goes farther back than I know you. If you speak not too fast, my mother can understand. If I see he does not, I will explain in Ojibway."

So it was Celestina's turn. She told them of sunny, hot Mexico and its mountains. She described Monterey, where she had lived. She detailed their trip to Michigan, crowded in a huge truck, and their life in the beet fields. Her descriptions were of occurrences, common enough to everyone, but strange to the Big Johns, who were unused to the most ordinary customs of older, settled communities. The thing Celestina stressed most was the three years she had spent in the big University hospital. Her parents had remained in Michigan one winter, and because she had wanted to learn to speak English she had attended the nearest rural school. There she had been examined by a doctor and nurse and they had suggested to her father that she should come in to the town to the tuberculosis clinic. They had advised her to go to the University hospital for treatment, and after they had explained why she should go, and had persuaded her father to allow her to leave his home, she had been willing to comply.

For three years they had kept her there, and during that time she had learned to like the hospital and the doctors and nurses. She had learned to speak English, and had been taught to read, to write well, and to sew and mend. She had been dismissed from the hospital, finally, but she was to wear her brace for two years longer. Then the doctor and nurse had advised her younger Sister, Antonio, to go to the same hospital, for she also had tuberculosis. She had demurred violently, stubbornly shaking her long, silky braids at them as she refused their suggestions and coaxings. Finally she had consented to go, but her decision had been too late, and she had never returned to them. Celestina's voice became thick, and she stopped suddenly in her story.

Then Jim again took-up the tale and held them fascinated. He described for them the huge oil derricks and the oil fields. They had driven through them at night when they started north, and the great flares of burning gas had lighted the whole countryside as if a hundred houses were all burning simultaneously. Supper time came and went, and still they sat enthralled with this story of another world than theirs. The sweeping wind and the pouring rain were unheard. Celestina looked at Kahnee and laughed aloud at the rapt expression on her face. "Oh, I am so hungry, Ka-ah-nee," she said. "There will be all winter to finish telling this story. Let's get something to eat. I will help, and you will see that I am good for something around a house."

Again she put her arm around Kahnee, casually, naturally as an affectionate sister would do, and almost lightheartedly Kahnee went with her to the kitchen. When the story broke off and the girls closed the door behind them, Big John wondered if Jennie and Joe Pete would leave such an interesting place as Jim had described and return to them again, and if he might possibly have been too sure in his belief that they would. Uncertainty began to grow in his mind.

As Celestina was that first day, so they found her all winter. She was pliable and eager to learn their customs and how they did things. She made friends easily, but was always steadfast in her allegiance to Kahnee. Always there was laughter on her lips and a quip in answer to discouragements. Some of her questions were comical and others seemed to the Indians unanswerable, because they had never been asked before. At the end of the first month, when she asked Big John why all the other families did not have piles of stove wood ready for the winter as he did, and just what they did when they had no wood, he had to rub his hair all endwise in his usual way and answer that he did not know, he had never thought of it. When she questioned them about the size of their farms, their farm machinery, what crops they raised and how high their taxes were, he could only reply that Indians did not know very well how to farm, and asked her, in turn, what farm machinery they should have. Then Big John finally ended his puzzled discomfort and also her questions by telling her that when Joe Pete returned from the Indian School he would teach them all those things, reassuring himself, as he made this positive statement, that it was true.

In October, which turned into a blue-gold month of haze and sun after the winds and rains of September, Kahnee, Celestina and Madeline roamed the Island like gypsies. Kahnee put aside her basket weaving for the entire month, and all three girls, though they definitely typified the differences of the three races to which they belonged, experienced an unwonted freedom and harmony of spirit in those last days of Madeline with them, for she and Telesphore were leaving for Chicago early in November. Madeline had never seen Kahnee so animated, and wondered why she had never seen this phase of the Indian girl during all the months she had been visiting at the Big John Cabin. Poignant moments came to her that October, when Madeline wondered how she was going to leave this dream-like beauty of the Island for the noise of a big city and the endless clatter of voices, and ever endure it again. As she waited for the girls at the fork of some trail where they had decided to meet, she would sit motionless and absorbed, and at last become so conscious of the woods-sounds and colors and fragrances that she came to feel she would leave part of herself there in the woods when she went away.

In November Celestina was enlightened and a little frightened at the fact that though the younger Indians might accept her and her customs, the older ones never would change. She had suggested to Kahnee that they should have a Thanksgiving Day dinner. The Big Johns had never observed the day, and Celestina offered to prepare the entire meal, just as she had learned to do on the farm where she had worked. Then, when the meal was ready, Mrs. Big John had quietly refused to eat, after her first taste of the food. She was courteous, as usual, but she did not like food cooked in "new" fashion, and Big John ruefully agreed with her in her decision. He preferred Indian cooking, and also refused to eat this different-tasting food. Celestina was hurt, but she laughed and offered to help Kahnee cook something else which they could eat. When Big John looked at her, rather abashed because she was so good-natured about it, she laughed again, this time with sincerity. "That is all right, Father Big John," she soothed. "My own parents like food cooked with peppers like this, and so did the people on the big farm, but they would refuse to eat food that I might fix as Kahnee does." So the incident passed pleasantly because of her tact, but it started Celestina wondering whether the Indians would accept new customs as readily as her own people did. An event which happened later convinced her that they never would, that because a thing had always been done in a certain way until it had become a tradition; they would not change. To them the old conventions were best.

  In December, just after the Christmas celebration at the schoolhouse, Mrs. Vargatte became sick. Everyone thought she had caught a cold, but she did not get better. Mr. Vargatte brought doctors down from town, two trained nurses took charge of the house and sick-room, and no one was allowed to visit her, even for a moment. Armand came home, and for two weeks did not stir from the house and store. When he finally came over to see the Big Johns, he told them that the doctors had advised that his mother should be removed to a city hospital if they wanted her to get well again. He was too worried to talk about his school or anything but his mother, and the Big Johns caught his fear. He told them he had just come over to greet them and at the same time say farewell, for he and his father were leaving in the morning with the nurses and his mother. They had decided to take her to Detroit to a sanatorium, and she would not return for two or three months. Abe was to be left in complete charge of the store, and after Mrs. Vargatte was settled and everything arranged, Theophile would come back. Armand's school was close enough so he could go to visit his mother once each month. The fast train could take him the distance over-night. He was so absorbed in his own woes that he hardly noticed Celestina. Big John shook his head gloomily when they said goodbye. "They do so-strange thing in those big 'ospital," he commented. "They cut ---" Noticing that Celestina was listening and ready to weep, he stopped abruptly, for he suddenly remembered that she had spent three long years in just such a hospital, and that she, too, had come to love Mrs. Vargatte.

Then Celestina unconsciously tested him, not with any purpose of testing but because she wanted Mrs. Big John to have the same chance Mrs. Vargatte was having, of efficient diagnosis and care. "Father Big John," she said quietly, "Mother is really sick. Each month she grows a little bit weaker. She is just as sick as Mrs. Vargatte is, but in a different way. You say she is better in the summer, but she should not have to be sick all winter if we could know what is the matter with her. Something must be very wrong, or her feet would not swell so big, and she would have some strength. She must sit in her chair most of the time. A doctor could tell you what her trouble is and what to do for her. I do not know how it is here, but where I was in the state, if a person can't pay he can have a doctor for nothing. Maybe it could be arranged here. Will you take her to a doctor and see what is her trouble? Or will you let me ask the doctor who is coming down tomorrow for Mrs. Vargatte, to come and look at her?"

She thought she must have over-stepped or seriously offended him, because he sat for a long time without speaking. Then he said, laboriously in English, so she would understand. "He would not go, Cel'steen. He would not go. He will take the medicine of the Very Oldest 'Oman, but he will take no medicine from these strange white doctor. For Madame Vargatte it is well, but not for Indian 'oman. It is no use to talk more. He is 'fraid of white man's magic, and will do only w'at he is use to do."

"But Father Big John, she will do anything for you," the girl begged. "Won't you ask her just to let the doctor look at her? Maybe she is not eating the right food, and Ka-ah-nee and I could cook other things for her if the doctor would tell us." She turned toward Kahnee, where she sat weaving. "'Couldn't we fix good things for her, Ka-ah-nee?" she coaxed.

Big John did not wait for Kahnee to answer, however. Again he shook his head. "It is no good," he reiterated, "He would not go, and he would not have no doctor look at him. He is use to the old way, and he will not change. Indian 'oman use only Indian medicine."

Kahnee came over to Celestina and took her hand "Come," she said" and led the girl upstairs.

Celestina sat in the low chair and wiped the tears from her eyes, while Kahnee stood and watched her with a speculating look in her fathomless eyes. "Why won't he ask her to go, Ka~ah-nee?" Celestina pleaded. "It is not wrong surely, to wish someone you love to be cured!"

Kahnee shook her head and Celestina for a few seconds saw the deeply quiet reserve and cold aloofness which was the real Indian. Then, noticing the black eyes looking at her so intently, Kahnee smiled warmly, as she would at a child who had asked unwittingly an unethical question. "Do not ask our father too much, little sister. He cannot always answer, and he is already overworried about our mother. He believes he can some day take on all the ways of the whites, but that day will not come to my father, or to my mother. It may not come to me, either, for certain things I cannot make myself do, which go against the old traditions. We would rather have things go wrong because we keep the old ways than go right in a new way which is not ours. Jennie knows this and that is why she wants to stay away from us, and I believe she is influencing Joe Pete also not to return. That will break my father. Maybe you too will want to go, and will hate our customs as Jennie does, for you are a merry child, and you need happiness as another needs food. Come to me or Jim with your questions and we will answer them, but do not ask our father again. It is not good that his belief he can change is put to the trial. Never have I spoken so long to anyone before, but I would speak even longer to save my father from too much worry."

Celestina promised, and Kahnee knew she would keep faith. Hand in hand they went down the stairs and into the kitchen together to prepare the evening meal. Big John and Jane Big John watched them as they passed through the living room, then looked at each other, relieved. "Our Kahnee is our best girl, and beautiful," the mother whispered then to Big John.

Startled, he looked sidewise at her and pondered over the strange thing she had said, rubbing his hair to wild disorder. Then he understood and assented gravely. "You are right. Kahnee is our best daughter, and our most beautiful one. And Cel'steen is good, too."

CHAPTER XI
JENNIE

A FLAG, USED TO DECORATE A GRAVE

JENNIE

Again Jennie was home for the Summer vacation, and because of Celestina's presence things had gone smoothly. Though Celestina never for a moment neglected Kahnee, or made her feel left out of any pleasure or companionship, she and Jennie had much in common to chatter about, and many were the questions she plied Jennie with about the farm she used to live upon, which was near the Indian School land, and the people they both knew. Then, too, the Strange Woman had had a queer "spell" just before Jennie's return, and the girls made a daily trip to her cabin. For a long time the Strange Woman had sat, once again inert and listless, and without the unceasing care of the Indians she and the Child would probably have starved, for she had no thought of preparing food, though it lay before her on the table. Each day the girls brought baskets of food to her, or cooked what was already left by friends there in the small shanty in which these two alien ones dwelt. Sometimes Kahnee accompanied them, but she preferred to remain at home with her mother who tottered when she attempted to walk and who needed someone with her constantly. Jennie and Celestina loved the Child and delighted in combing her coppery, curling hair and caring for her. Despite the hardness which seemed to have become part of Jennie since she had left the Island, her sincere love for the Child had apparently remained with her.

Though Jennie had seemed glad to be with them again and had apparently settled down into the old routine of life in their fashion willingly enough, she constantly informed them, almost with defiance, that she was returning to the Indian School when September came again, and after she had finished the work there she planned to attend another school where she could continue in higher work. Some of her instructors had told her she might become a teacher in one of the western Indian schools, and she was more enthusiastic about that prospect than in anything else they could suggest. There was something so intangibly secret about her, as if she were not telling the entire truth, and she was so unusually emphatic when she vowed she would return to the school, that Big John looked at her wonderingly when he had time to think about her at all. They had not denied her the privilege of returning, yet she seemed to have an inner unease, as if she dreaded that they might do so. Always they smiled at her vehemence, and waited patiently for her ideas to change after she had adjusted herself to the Indian life again. Their attitude made her more than ever determined, and nothing Kahnee or Jim could argue moved her from that resolution. They discovered that it was wiser not to attempt to dissuade her, for if there was too much contradiction to her plans she shirked her duties at home and spent most of her day with the Strange Woman and the Child. It seemed as if she realized a wider freedom away from her own tribe and family, and in the cabin of the Strange Woman she indulged to the utmost her passion for doing things in the "new" ways, undeterred by family remonstrance and rebukes for forsaking their own habits and customs. The Strange Woman never interfered with any of her methods, and in that small cabin she felt released from the queer restlessness which constantly gripped her now and sometimes threatened her happiness. She was instinctively fastidious, and since she had lived away from her people for two years, their houses seemed slovenly and, at times, even dirty. She resented the fact that the corners of the living room must always be filled with untidy piles of basket timber of all colors, so her mother could more easily reach for it, and the litter which resulted from half-finished baskets sitting around the room, awaiting the last touches of her mother's skillful fingers, angered her. She was fiercely resentful when great clumps of dirt were tracked in from the trail on rainy days by the careless men of her family, and by guests also, upon her freshly scrubbed floors. She hated the eternal three-times-a-day diet of potatoes, onions and fish or meat, always cooked in the same way. She rebelled against the antagonistic attitude assumed by the family when she attempted to change their manners of living and eating, and their refusal to eat vegetables which she had learned to like at the School, and, because she was so pitifully young and inexperienced, did not realize that it was impossible to make such changes overnight in a people of unchanging traditions. Neither did she know that their attitude was not so much antagonistic as puzzled. She was quieted and pleased when the Strange Woman ate anything she was offered, without comment or demur, and though Jennie realized fully that this was an apathetic acquiescence, she was relieved to be in another cabin.

At times she even went over to the lodge left by Jerry for herself and Joe Pete when they should be married, and spasmodically cleaned that lonely place of its winter debris and great, wide-flung cobwebs which hung in lace-like dust-film from rafter to rafter. Sometimes Celestina joined her in these excursions, and they had impromptu picnics there where they could cook and eat what they chose. At those times the two girls were drawn close together in a rather peculiar friendship which had as its basis their unacknowledged loneliness and their mutual feeling about conditions in their own home and in other homes on the Island. Not a word of criticism was openly spoken by either at those intimate times, they were too loyal for that, but occasionally, when Mrs. Big John quietly but stubbornly refused to allow Jennie to buy the groceries or do any of the cooking, or refused to eat some special tid-bit which Jennie had painstakingly prepared for her in a swift, involuntary glance at Celestina she would find a mute sympathy in the Mexican girl's black eyes, and knew that Celestina was sorry for her because she had already had the same experience. Jennie had not the kindly patience of Celestina, and her irritation constantly grew, until by the end of the summer it had consummated in a relentless decision to get away from the Island somehow, no matter how ill her mother might be, and a resolution that she would never return to their cabin until their attitude had changed. She had gone out from the Island to escape, it was true, but she had also sincerely wished to learn the white man's ways of living. Now her own people were denying her the privilege of using that learning, which they had professed to want, to alleviate or improve the conditions under which they were slowly deteriorating. They would not accept her suggestions in caring for wounds or accidents, but used the herbs and brews of the Very Oldest Mother, and laughed at her attempts to teach them the theories of sanitation. They had always done very well without them, so they would continue to do without them. The obstinate unreasonableness and unfairness of their attitude made her rather hopeless, and with this feeling of failure came a greater feeling of impatience and an uncertainty of temper. What she had prophesied to Madeline the previous summer that she believed the reaction of her people would be had become an actual fact which she was encountering, and she could see no way out of the dilemma unless a stranger to them all offered a solution to the problem. She still did not believe Madeline's theory that young people of all races encountered that same difficulty when they tried to force, too suddenly, alien customs upon old people who loved their own ways; and that in every new change something beautiful, intangible, never to be reclaimed, and which only the sensitive could understand, was lost when the old was too suddenly discarded.

When the letter came to Big John from the Indian School and she read it aloud to her father at his request, she would not believe what the words said there, under her own eyes. All summer she had refused to believe it, but this letter was confirmation. The information which the superintendent wanted Big John to have was clearly and concisely stated, so there could be no misunderstanding, and corroborated what the teachers had ventured to hint to her before she had left the School. The "Government," always an impersonal, intangible thing to the Indians, had decided to close the Indian School and place the Indian children in other schools with white children. Unless a child had no parents he could not return to the school, and then only temporarily. Jennie scanned the letter twice before she could read it to Big John, and then she recited it automatically as though she were not conscious of the actual meaning of the words she was speaking to him from the official-looking paper she held so stiffly in her fingers. But underneath her apparent stoicism, all of her was hurting intolerably, and her mind was already frantically seeking a way out. She had experienced two years of better conditions of living, she had been immaculately clean and well-housed, and she could not return to the old life again. If they would only allow her to modify certain habits to which they clung so tenaciously she would not have minded too greatly, but she could not put behind her all she had learned of sanitation, ordered living, and books, and live as she had with them when she was a child. She did not dare to look at her father because of the distaste he would read in her eyes, and Big John could only stare at her when she concluded and ask her if she had read correctly, if someone had made a mistake. The written word would never lose its magic for him, but even magic sometimes errs. In reply, Jennie again read the letter, slowly, carefully, studying every word for its full meaning, and after the second perusal they knew what she had read first was final. The plan the superintendent suggested was that Joe Pete should go immediately to the school he and Big John had discussed, and that Jennie should attend one of the local Island schools. Big John looked deep into her dazed eyes, then turned and stared out of the window, apparently as immobile and uncaring as a wooden man. At last he understood what had bothered her all summer. He would not look again at the pain he saw in those eyes, and he had nothing to offer her, in consolation or in mitigation of her misery. It was true he could not understand her wild desire to go away from a place in which she had been happy enough, but neither could he sympathize with her frustrated hopes. Not once did it occur to him that by acceptance of her new learning he could make life on the Island bearable for her. Nor could she entertain the idea that she could plead with him to do so. After all, she was only a woman, and women had no authority in tribal matters. All he could suggest was that she could go to the Island school if she wished, but she refused to talk with him. She flung out of the cabin and started swiftly down the trail to Vargatte's, and Big John's aching worry about her was somewhat eased when he noted the direction she went.

She reached the store and asked for Mrs. Vargatte, so absorbed in her own troubles that she had forgotten Mrs. Vargatte had not been home long from the hospital in the city. The nurse told her Delima was resting and would not allow her to go into the room. Theophile, knowing the girl would not ask to see his wife unless her dilemma was serious, finally shook his head dubiously, over-rode the authority of the nurse, and told her she might go in for a few minutes. But when Jennie sat by Delima's bed and saw those tired eyes looking at her from the white face and looked at the delicate fingers which clung weakly and sympathetically to hers, she could not burden Mrs. Vargatte with her difficulties. She forced herself to smile and went softly from the room. And Delima was so feeble that she could not insist that Jennie must tell her what the problem was, and wept at her new uselessness to her friends.

Jennie had never faced an afternoon of such alternate hope and despondency. She was like a small frantic child which has unexpectedly lost its way. Over her surged wild rebellion at her lot, and under its lash she walked swiftly and wept despairingly. Then a sense of futility and hopelessness would come upon her, accompanied by a sick feeling in the pit of her stomach, and she would drop flat by the side of the trail and simply endure it, with closed eyes and clenched fists until it passed. For the first time she experienced mental trouble which sickened her physically also. Finally she knew she must go home, with her problem unsolved, because, for all her thinking and weeping there was no solution to it. Dusk was thickening the afternoon shadows when she passed under the ancient oak tree and turned into their own narrow trail, walking home as listlessly as the Strange Woman might have done. Celestina ran to her, but Jennie shook her off. "I had forgot Mrs. Vargatte was so sick, me, and went to visit with her," she said, and they nodded and accepted that as an explanation for her afternoon's absence.

Celestina was patient but not stoical, even in front of people. Her race was more emotional and they had not hesitated to express their feelings unrestrainedly. She could never become accustomed to this stolidity of her new family. Her heart was wrung for Jennie, and she could not forbear offering such sympathy as she was able. She disappeared upstairs. They heard her rummaging among her things, and after a time she returned to the living room with a gorgeous shawl hung over her arms, trailing its long fringe behind her on the floor like a silken train. "This is for you, Jennie," she said. "It was in my box and I had forgotten it. My mother had it from a lady she worked for in Monteray, and though it is not new now it is still beautiful. My mother gave it to me when I married Jim."

The shawl was indeed beautiful. None of them had ever seen anything which could compare with it, though the material of it was cracked with age. It was of a soft yet heavy, red slippery silk which felt as cool and smooth as quicksilver running through the fingers. On this gay background were embroidered flowers of every conceivable color and design, all blending into a subtle beauty which was, to these Indian women, miraculous. They found it difficult to believe that women of another race had done such intricate work with needles and silk threads, but Celestina assured them that Mexican women were adept in such work. Even Jennie for a time forgot her sorrow. She was overwhelmed by Celestina's generosity, for she knew Celestina loved color as poignantly as she did, and this was a garment that any woman would covet greedily. Jennie was sure that if the shawl had been hers originally, no matter how worn it might become, she could never bear to part with it. When Kahnee smoothed it wishfully with her great rough hands, Jennie almost snatched it from her.

"You wear it so," explained Celestina, laughing excitedly. "The great lady who gave it to my mother wore hers like this; and she was beautiful, and no fairer in color than we are, and she said the shawl must always be allowed to fold itself as it wished about a woman's body."

As she spoke she stood and wrapped the shawl about her with one dexterous twist. It draped over one shoulder and hung in folds of loveliness about her. She pirouetted on one heel and instantly became a whirl-wind of color. As she slowed again, the long fringe swirled against her ankles, softly and with graceful beauty. "Isn't it pretty, Jennie? I want you to have it, and you will wear it to the party in the Hall next month, and you will be the prettiest girl there. So come, and let me show you how it folds about you!"

But during the next few weeks, even the glamor of the Mexican shawl could not solace Jennie. She could not force herself to sit still for long at a time, and was constantly moving about, so aimlessly most of the time that her mother became also restless and disturbed, just watching her. Jennie knew her mother was not strong and that her weakness was aggravated by her own display of emotion, so she remained away from the house as often and as long as she could provide a reasonable excuse. Jim was generous with his car. He had taught Jennie to drive, and whenever he was not using it she drove up and down the one long road on the Island. Sometimes she would park in some solitary spot by the road-edge and muse there unhappily on what she had wished to do, and try to evolve some plan which would enable her to get away. When no solution came to her she drove recklessly, easing her grief solely through the swift motion of the car.

Finally one day she left the childishness of hope and dreams behind her and gave up planning, for she admitted to herself at last that only help from someone who could afford to pay her expenses would get her out of the situation. She knew no such person. They lived only in stories she had read. She had not enough learning to enable her to work for any white person and the path to further knowledge had been closed to her. She wanted more than the Island rural school could offer. Her dreams must end, for she had to remain on the Island. She must face an ugly reality of hard work, early old age, and a life of few comforts. She knew for the first time a realization of the value of money, which most Indians never know. She asked the eternal question of the why of life's unequal distribution of wealth, and could neither answer the question herself nor obtain a satisfactory explanation from her friends, who could not understand why she would want more than they had and were quite satisfied to possess. A queer, ineluctable desperation dropped upon her spirit then, and she did not seem to care what happened, even to those she had really loved. She snatched an empty happiness and fun wherever she could find it, and did not feel any remorse if that snatching took the joy from others.

So things went on until the night of the big dance in the Hall. For Jennie's sake the family had planned carefully so the girls could go. Jim and Big John had an errand far down at that end of the Island where the Hall was located, but they decided to walk and leave the car at the cabin for the girls. They knew a short-cut through the woods which would cut the distance in half. In the evening, after the men had finished their work, they would tramp over to the Hall. Young John and Moses were coming over from the dredge-job, which was not too far away, and they would meet at the party. When the dance was over they would all drive home, for Big John had been coaxed into promising that he would stay for the dance. Jim cautioned Jennie to drive carefully, and with her promise he and her father were content, and started down the trail to their work. They turned at the big oak, a never-forgotten custom, and saluted Mrs. Big John, who watched them from the window. She turned away then and continued her weaving. She was intent on this basket, for it was a special order, made of extra-fine splints, of blue and gold colors, and trimmed with sweet-grass. Celestina stared even after the men had gone from sight. She could still see them standing there like brown statues; their right arms raised high in courteous farewell. She could not become accustomed to certain gracious things they did. She mused until Jennie called her to come and see about her dress for the evening.

All afternoon the two girls fussed and laughed over their wardrobes and what they should wear at the party. Kahnee did not want to go, but she was as interested as they in what their final decision would be. It was Celestina's first Island dance and her excitement was contagious. Mrs. Big John smilingly offered the purple dress which Telesphore had brought and which was as good as new. The girls laughed as they replied that they could wrap it around both of them and have enough material left for scarfs. The mother laughed and nodded and bent over her grass-braiding. She was surrounded by an aura of its tantalizing, elusive odor. When she looked up again, Celestina was lovely and almost exotic in her gay green wedding dress. Jennie wanted to wear an orange colored dress, but changed to blue at the last minute because the shawl looked better with that color.

At last they were ready. Celestina wore her old coat and Jennie was well wrapped in the shawl, which they pinned about her so it would cover her arms, even though it hampered her movements. The nights had already become cold, but the girls preferred to drive with the car windows lowered. They loved the wind blowing crisply on their faces as they raced down the road. They called gay farewells when they climbed into the seat and started the car. It sputtered and growled at first at Jennie's erratic procedure, but it slid smoothly out of the yard and on to the trail, leaving behind it a comet's tail of dust. When they turned at the oak tree, they blew the horn raucously in a last goodbye to Kahnee and Mrs. Big John, and drove on laughing. They knew how their mother would shake her head in disapproval at their racket, which was breaking the twilight silence she loved, and their parody of farewell. For this once they took an elfish delight in her condemnation. They were sure of having an amusing time at this dance and they refused to have any unpleasantness or sorrow riding along with them.

They stopped at the store and went in on an entirely unnecessary errand. They knew they were young and beautiful and had a childish delight in "showing off" their party clothes. For just a moment they ran in to say good evening to Delima Vargatte and break the monotony of her day. They rejoiced over her fluent compliments and then were on their way again, having passed on to Delima some of their happiness. Envious youngsters gazed longingly after them as Jennie turned the car and started off to the party.

Celestina had never seen Jennie so excited. At every word they said, she giggled, and her wit was keenly brilliant. Celestina thought she was like one "possessed." The distance seemed very short. When their lights outlined a huge pine tree, Jennie realized they were very close to the abrupt turn above the high hill which was only a few miles from the Hall. Suddenly the car struck some large obstacle which had been dropped in the road, probably from a wood-wagon, and the resulting bump left the girls laughing and breathless. But the long shawl had somehow become entangled around Jennie's foot and the brake pedal, and the strong silken fringe had twined snakily through her fingers and around the steering wheel. When she vainly attempted to loosen her hands, the cords cut into her fingers and held tenaciously. Terror came upon her with the realization that she could not make the turn, for they would be upon it instantly and she had no control over the car. She had time only to call in a terrified voice a warning to Celestina, who was arranging her own rumpled wraps, entirely unaware of what was ahead of them. As she shouted, they struck the huge pine. The impact was terrific. Great strips of bark flew into the air as the car cut into the tree and climbed against it. The girls were thrown through the windows, and there was a soft, horrible swoosh as their bodies hit and skidded across the packed sand. One scream of agony tore through the quiet of the night. The car lights went out and there was a metallic rattling as it fell from its upright position and rolled on its side, settling there with small creaking noises which soon ceased. Where a moment before had been screaming and shock was now only thick night and silence. But in that moment Something had gone out into the Black and over the End's Edge.

After a long time Celestina awoke from a nightmare dream of torment and whimpered a little when that dream became reality. For a while she could not remember where she was or what had happened to them. She tried to move, but the pain was too great for endurance, so she lay quiet, trying hard to stop those involuntary moans which apparently were coming from her own lips. Her mind worked hazily. She was back in Mexico, and her mother was calling her to wake and come to breakfast. She was working on the sugar-beet farm, and her entire body was aching from stooping hour after hour to weed the beets. A stinging pain shot through her, and she remembered. She had been going to the big dance. She had been laughing about something. There had been a great crash. She put her hand to her head, which ached unbearably, and felt a warm stream of blood running across her forehead. Her hand was sticky when she rubbed it upon her coat, and she continued to rub it there, almost foolishly thinking as she did so that her coat would be spoiled and they could not afford to buy another. Her left arm was doubled under her in such an awkward, unnatural fashion that she realized it must be broken. Her body was numb and, though she willed with all her strength to move the broken arm into a more comfortable position, she could not. Suddenly she remembered Jennie. She called her name over and over, "Jennie! Jennie! O Jennie!" but Jennie did not answer. Again she tried to move and her mind seemed to fall into a black pit, so she was forced to remain where she had been thrown. After many endless minutes she dozed and was unconscious of pain or fear for Jennie.

There, at the roots of the big wounded pine, Big John, Young John, Moses and Jim found them when they came searching, knowing that some accident had befallen. When Big John's lantern lighted the tree and he saw it stripped of its bark almost to its first high limb, he gasped and could look no more. He handed the lantern to the boys, turned away from them all, and sat there on the hill waiting for their report. They found Jennie not far from the tree. She was dead. When they discovered how horribly she was hurt they were thankful she had been killed almost instantly. Celestina's feeble, continuous moans told them she was living, but they did not dare to move her until help came. The car was worthless. Finally, men arrived and helped to carry both girls back to the Settlement. They left Jennie there in one of the Indian homes which was offered them for her. Celestina they carried to the Big John cabin, and Mrs. Vargatte's doctor told them that when her broken arm mended and the great cut on her head healed, he believed she would be entirely well again. The bruises on her body, though they were painful, were not serious.

Mrs. Big John sat stolidly while the strange white doctor talked with them, but her eyes were tragic. When he had gone to Vargatte's for breakfast, she turned to Big John. "I could not understand his words," she whispered, "they were so many and strange ones without meaning. Where is our Jennie? Was she so hurt that she could not be carried to her home?"

Big John could not answer. He was aghast at what had come to them now. First his Waubegoon! Now Jennie! He was sore, and puzzled, and deeply wondering. Jim looked at them both, and knew the burden of speech was now his. Typically Indian, he could not soften the news. It had to be imparted with one deep stab. "Jennie was too terribly hurt, my mother. She is dead."

Mrs. Big John's head dropped. She muttered, more to herself than to them, exactly what Big John was wondering. "Why has this bad medicine been put upon us? Who is so deadly an enemy to us? First my Small Flower and now Jennie. I am old and the end of my Trail is close. Why must their Trail be shortened that they cannot be with us when we step from ours? Aih-ah, Big John, life is too hard for us. Never again shall I see them smiling or coming in through our door!"

She sat there in the big rocker, too weary for tears, trying desperately to fit the old habit of stoicism to this fresh hurt. Kahnee looked at her and nodded sadly. "It seems that the life of the Indian becomes harder all the time, my mother dear." Her eyes filled. "I too shall miss them, mother. But it was this comfortless life which made our Jennie desire to get away from the Island. Her mind was so full of trouble about this thing, that as long as she got away she did not care how it came about. Was there one moment of great gladness at her release, do you think, just before she went out into the Black?"

It was a long time before anyone answered. Then the old mother spoke, though her voice was barely audible. "Yes, Kahnee. Jennie wanted greatly to leave the Island, as you say. And possibly we did not help her, so she may have been happy to know she was going. But I wanted her here with us. Now she has gone away from the Island, far away from us! I cannot be glad she had her desire!"

Upstairs, Celestina was very ill. She was homesick too. If she were home now, so bruised and weak, her mother would have hovered constantly at her side, crooning soft little love-words that in themselves would have eased the pain. Here, even Jim did not seem to care. Would she always be an alien even though she had come to love these people? Would they always remain "shut up" and reserved? She sobbed uncontrollably, and Kahnee and Jim heard her through their mother's mourning. They glanced at each other quickly, and both started up the stairs. They did not hurry and there were no crooning love-words from them when they entered the room. But they came! Kahnee patted her hand and sat in a chair close to her bed to talk quietly with her. Jim leaned over her and straightened the covers, and she knew that underneath his silence was also his lasting love for her. She forced herself to calmness, and resolved that she would be merry and truly happy in this household as long as she stayed in it. They had suffered too, but they would be glad she was here. She reached for a hand of each, and without embarrassment they held hers, and sat in silence as was seemly. Their bond of friendship deepened and strengthened into an understanding beyond the need of words, and now Celestina knew why they were a reticent race.

Downstairs, Big John suddenly ceased rubbing his hair all endwise. He had not found the answer to their questioning, but he had made a resolution. He turned to his wife and said simply, but with finality, "It is indeed hard, Jane. Each year our troubles grow heavier and our strength to carry them becomes less. But we are Indian, and so, we go on!"

CHAPTER XII
THE FOREIGNER

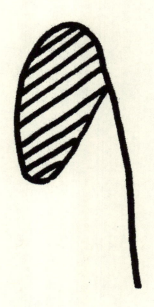

A FLAG, USED TO MARK A GRAVE

THE FOREIGNER

The wind drifted slowly across the brown fields, prodding the grass into lazy motion; blue clintonia fruits and vermillion bunchberries bordered the brown trails; birds sang in the woods; and massed white clouds crossed the sky; but the Strange Woman would never hear or see these things again. She was dead. Big John had asked Willyum Wauswahgun, pseudo-carpenter of the Island, to come to her house and help fashion a coffin from the smooth, bird's-eye maple boards that Mr. Vargatte had given him two years earlier to make cupboards for Jane Big John, and which Big John had never had time to build. As the two men worked, Big John told Willyum as much as he himself knew. He had found her the preceding day in the cabin when he had gone with a pack-sack of food for her and the Child. Mary Shaganaubegon had stopped in at the Big John house and had told them that the Strange Woman was acting queerly, even more so than usual, as if she were newly terrified by something she did not attempt to explain, and had refused to speak to Mary when she, as usual, had gone in on her way from town to admire the Child. In fact, the Strange Woman had not seemed to realize that Mary was standing before her and asking questions about the way she felt, and her eyes appeared to be filmed and sunken in her head.

Big John was worried and had started out immediately for the home of the Strange Woman. Old Green-Cloud's personality had faded from the place since she had become its tenant. The day was cold, with the smell and feel of autumn in the brake-scented, crisp air, yet when he reached Green Cloud's clearing where the old, picturesque cabin hugged the ground, he saw no smoke rising from the chimney. Big John listened at the door and, to his relief, heard Deneece laughing within. Gently he called, then courteously waited a moment or two, and receiving no answer, pushed the door open and entered. Through the door space a long beam of sunlight slipped beside him into the room and fell upon the Child, playing happily on the floor with a big yellow hairpin which Mary

Shaganaubegon bad given her. With cries of ecstasy she held the transparent celluloid thing up in the light streaming through the doorway, and it shone as though she had actually caught and held in her hand a piece of the sun itself. She made love-sounds to the shining pin, and Big John almost involuntarily crossed himself, though he had become accustomed to the sight of the Child ignoring everything else and playing with the pin ever since Mary had given it to her more than a year previously. She would not be parted from it for a moment, and was contented anywhere if she had it with her. Because of her love for it, the pin had taken on, for the Indians, some of the magic they associated with the Child. Now she was amusing herself peacefully with it while the Strange Woman lay upon the bed in the corner, apparently asleep. There was a pile of wood near the stove, where some passing Indian had stacked it for her. But no fire had been built that morning and no food was on the table. Big John felt queer. He came close to the bed and looked at the motionless Woman, and knew immediately that she was dead. Her lips were tipped up at the corners in a half-smile, as if an amusing memory from a happier time than she had known on the Island had finally solaced her in her last moment.

As Big John and Willyum discussed it, stopping occasionally to admire an unusual marking in the boards they were cutting, the Child played unconcernedly near them, wandering in and out of the cabin as she pleased. They stared at her, and even from their stolidity was forced a comment of keen appreciation of her beauty, natural as sunshine. Each year her hair had become more golden than red, like shafts of tangible amber light which had been caught and twined around one's finger, keeping the curve of it. The shining mass of curls hung below her waist, and every tiny breeze shimmered it into waves of indescribable loveliness of texture. She was an elfin, fairy-like child. Her eyes were happy ones, even though they were as empty blue as a cloudless summer sky. She probably would never learn to talk, they realized, but she laughed with odd little chucklings to herself. When the men noticed her standing with her exquisite head bent over some brightly colored flower, they unfailingly repeated to each other that she was listening intently to whisperings of Manitou, who spoke with her in such a way, through the medium of birds and flowers, that only she could hear and understand. White people would always say that she was "not right," but the Indians loved her with a reverent, worshiping adoration, for Manitou had touched her mind and thus set her apart from other human beings. As soon as the Woman was buried, Big John planned to take the Child to his home permanently. Mrs. Big John and Celestina had begged him to do this, and Kahnee had more deliberately agreed with them that he should. Again Willyum and Big John discussed the mystery of the appearance of the Strange Woman, and wondered if they would ever discover more about her than they now knew; and underneath all their talking was the unexpressed foreboding that some day they would lose the Child also. So that premonition might not be expressed in words and thus become a reality, they changed the topic to Willyum's work, and planned for the next week, when he would return to his job towing pulpwood for a man who lived over on the mainland. He was to use his auxiliary sailboat this fall, for the loads coming up the river were unusually heavy. Big John agreed to help him go over the caulking, and also see if the planks were sound.

Their conversation was abruptly interrupted, and at that moment there happened the strangest of all the strange coincidences that had ever occurred in the oral history of the tribe. Even as they were changing their conversation from the Child to Willyum's work, they saw coming into the clearing a huge yellow-haired man. He swaggered over to them and looked down at the box they were making. No one could look at it and not know what it was.

"Well! I'm too late and she's dead at last, is she!" he commented rather than asked. "Who are you fellows!"

"I'm Big John, me. She's Willyum Wauswahgun," answered Big John with quiet courtesy, keeping his eyes warily empty of amazement and incredulity.

"So you're the fellow who's the big shot on this Island," said the stranger insolently. "I'm Olafson, and I'm looking for my woman and kid."

Big John went rigid as he looked up with quick understanding into the cold blue eyes of the foreigner, and as he did so he felt a sudden surge of hatred fill him. He instantly remembered Mary's statement that the Strange Woman had seemed horror-struck and wondered now if perhaps there had been a reason. Behind the blue of Olafson's eyes, Big John was staring straight into the impenetrable blue ice of a northern glacier; into eyes which would never warm with any feeling of human kindness. Big John tried to look away, but was unable, for he realized that he had always been unsure of their possession of the Child and had unconsciously expected and awaited the appearance of a man like this one during the ten years that the Strange Woman and the Child had been theirs. It almost seemed as if the foreigner had watched them from a distance, invisible, but knowing their subconscious uneasiness, and had waited, or even been responsible for, this timely hour when he could appear without shouldering any of the burden of the two. Yet, Big John knew his suspicion was improbable and the whole occurrence must be one of those uncannily queer experiences that happen in the life of everyone; one of the unordinary events of existence which cannot be explained.

"When did she die?" asked Olafson. "Or is she really dead! Can't you fellows talk English?" His voice was like his eyes, and loud, as if by sheer tone-volume he could make them understand better what he said. He was ruthless, implacable, and would not wait long for anything he wanted.

Big John hated to tell him anything about the castaways who had for so long now been a real part of the tribe. But the Indian code does not allow interference in the family affairs of another, no matter what the provocation may be. A man owns his wife and children, and may do exactly as he wishes with them. So, pointing to the coffin they were making, Big John said reluctantly, "This we make for your 'oman."

"What happened to her?" the outlander wanted to know, but the Indians sensed a wariness behind the question. "We do not know, us," Big John answered. "When we pass yesterday we came in his house to bring him some food, and he's dead. Come with me and see him."

Olafson followed him into the cabin. There he looked down at the smiling face of the dead woman and cursed, obscenely. As Big John listened he was glad that the Strange Woman, even though it was through the black trail of death, had escaped this man, and understood how she might have had fear beaten into the fiber of her until even after she had lost all memory of the cause of the fear, it still was an integral part of her. He knew now why she constantly and furtively turned and looked over her shoulder as though the shadow of some brutal, plundering animal stood just behind her.

From the Woman the foreigner's attention slid to the Child, playing on the floor with her yellow hairpin. He saw that she had an eerie, ethereal perfection of features seldom seen except in the old master-painted portraits, and there came to him, almost as a shock, a quick realization of her uncommon beauty and what he might do with her. At what he saw leap into Olafson's eyes, Big John felt sick. He had seen it often before, in the eyes of many kinds of men, but never so foully. The man did not move his body, but reached out with unusually long arms and, hooking his fingers in her tangled curls, brutally yanked the Child toward him. It was the first unkindness the Child had ever experienced, although she had lived all her years with a supposedly unfeeling people. Olafson held her tightly between his knees and, still hanging cruelly to her hair, bent her face back into the beam of light and studied it closely. Her eyes, intensely blue in her colorless face, stared fixedly into his, but she did not cry out in fear or pain as another child would have done under the same harsh treatment. Big John realized she did not know how to cry; she had never had to learn the meaning of tears, or sorrow, or ugliness. Immediately Olafson knew she was a half-wit. He shoved her from him, and slumped into a chair near the bed.

"Get out for awhile," he said to Big John. "I want to think."

Big John went out of the cabin and sat again beside Willyum. They ostensibly resumed their work on the coffin, but Willyum could see that Big John was thinking hard and fast, and was nonplussed over a problem he must solve without too much time to think it through. Every few moments he removed his hat and rubbed his hair until it stood on end. This situation he had to work out alone and immediately, for he dare not leave the foreigner and the Child even long enough to ask Vargatte for advice. They worked until Olafson came from the house, closing the door behind him as if the Strange Woman and the Child might hear and understand what he said. He sauntered over to the men.

"You're right," he announced to Big John, who wondered dazedly what he had ever said to this man that was "right." "She was my woman. I thought I had her tamed, but she ran off with another fellow. Told him she was scared of me, and worked on his sympathy. When I got her back again I learned her something that I thought she would never forget."

Big John felt his spine tingle as he imagined what this man-brute had "learned" the Strange Woman. But he was still talking, and Big John did not want to miss a word of explanation.

"Then right away she got loony. And Frieda was born -- that's the girl's name there-- and I never knew what become of her and the kid. I wouldn't go after her the second time she went."

Though the foreigner looked with apparent frankness straight into Big John's eyes, the Indian studied his ruthless mouth and knew he was not telling the truth. But an Indian never contradicts, even when he knows the other person is boasting or lying.

"We find him on the shore, one long time ago," Big John put in a tentative claim, stalling for more time to plan; trying to find a way to out-maneuver this stranger.

"Maybe. But she was mine first," returned Olafson, and according to Indian ethics, Big John had to admit to himself that the fellow was within his rights. "And the kid is mine now," the foreigner continued. "So I'm taking her along back with me. What name have you Indians called her?"

Willyum spoke for the first time, proudly, as one did when he spoke of an important person. "Telesphore call him Deneece!"

"It's a hell of a name," growled Olafson, "but I guess it's fancier than Frieda, and a fancy name will be good for the trade."

"What you're goin' do wit' him?" asked Big John.

"I'll put you guys onto something," laughed Olafson, coldly, cruelly affable, "and if you've got any more good-looking, half-wit girls hanging round, Indian or white, you can use my tip, or I'll take them off your hands. I'll keep her a few more years and learn her to step lively when I tell her to do anything, no matter what it is. She's got to unlearn a lot, I can see right now, for you Indians have spoiled her. After I've trained her for two or three years, or maybe a little longer, she's going to earn an easy living for me."

"He have never work, livin' wit' us," said Big John. "He can't earn no money for he do not know how to work. He is only little girl; only use' to laugh and play. And he don' talk."

"All the better for her and me both that she don't talk. That'll be one thing I don't have to learn her not to do. Her work will be a snap," said Olafson, and again Big John had the feeling of ice behind his words. "Then when she ain't no good to me any more I'll put her in one of these state institutions. They're run by a gang of damn-fool, soft-hearted sob-sisters to care for such trash. Lots of places like that for crazy people if you want to put them in, and detention homes for stray girls that a kind and worried father can't do nothing with. A fellow can always work the gag if he knows how." He laughed contemptuously.

Willyum asked the question that Big John would not ask, breaking all rules of ethics with his inquiry. "What can that small one do to earning money for big fellow like you?"

Again the foreigner laughed. "I'll make her a damned street-walker," he answered, and his terseness was like a slap in their faces. "She's got the looks, and no wits to fight me or give me away. She's a gold-mine. She'll draw the fellows like flies. Her looks are that kind. There's money in her, handled right."

Willyum ventured another query, while Big John wondered at his effrontery. "He is your own girl and you do that to him?"

I don't know whether she's mine or not, but she was my woman's kid," answered Olafson. "She never got those looks off me! And I told you that her mother ran away with another fellow. She don't look like her mother, neither, when it comes to that. Anyway, I'm talking too much and wasting time. I'll get her and start now." Big John said nothing, but he watched every move the stranger made.

"We'll start right now." Olafson repeated, as if he expected some resistance from the two Indians, and went to the cabin to get the Child. He called her by name. "Dee'neece! Dee'neece! Come here, you, Dee'neece!"

The Child paid no attention to him.

"This is where you begin to learn right this minute, you devil's brat, that when I speak to you I mean business, and you'd better jump," he threatened, and grasping the Child by both small hands, jerked her violently upon her feet. She gave a queer little cry which made Big John squirm inside, and dropped again on the floor, hunting for the yellow hair-pin which had flown from her hands and fallen under the edge of the bed when Olafson had grabbed her. Again the foreigner seized her, shook her roughly and set her upright, this time striking her with his open hand across the face so hard that his fingers left their marks on her delicate skin. The Child gasped and her eyes became wild but she did not weep or repeat her cry. Big John had followed to the door and was watching. His face was set in ugly lines and his big fists clenched, but he spoke quietly. "He want his 'air-pin."

"Damn her hair-pin," yelled Olafson. He pushed the door as far as it would swing back on its hinges, once again stood the Child brutally on her feet, and went out, pulling her after him though she automatically braced herself and resisted him with all her frail strength. Big John bent slowly and picked up the yellow hair-pin. He gazed at it, thinking deeply for a few minutes while he held it carefully in his huge fingers, then dropped it into his pocket and left the room.

"Wait here until someone returns," he warned the carpenter, speaking in Indian. Willyum assented and continued his hammering.

Olafson glanced suspiciously at the men as they spoke the strange language, turned from them and hurried down the path toward the shore "What are you doing then, Big John?" asked Willyum as Big John waited long enough to allow Olafson to vanish from their sight.

But Big John did not hear the question, for he was swiftly following the trail behind the foreigner and the Child yet in spite of his speed, going silently as only Big John could go through the woods. He stayed within a certain distance of the two he was tracking. He was waiting without impatience for the sign to tell him he could interfere. From ahead came continual cries and the sound of blows, and in places on the path he could see where the Child had fought madly, like a small trapped animal. How long would the Great Spirit wait before giving an indication of his displeasure! Or did he expect Big John to act without a sign! The big Indian began to get anxious. He could not bear to wait much longer, even if this were the pleasure of Manitou, or a trial which Manitou was sending to him.

Suddenly from close in front of him came the sound of an oath. Then little, swift-running feet tore down the trail toward him. The Child was free! The sign had come! Big John knew Manitou wanted him to interfere. The bushes parted and the Child ran, panting and stumbling. Her face was flushed and her eyes stared, wide with fear. For a moment Big John dared to feel resentment that Manitou had too cruelly awakened her to feeling. As Deneece swerved to pass him, Big John reached down and gathered her in his arms as though she were of no weight at all. She screamed pitifully, in her terror not recognizing him, and as he muffled her mouth against his coat he felt her heart pounding. Gently he slipped the yellow hair-pin into her hand, and at the familiar feel of it she stopped crying and, clinging desperately to him, seemed to know that she was safe again with an old friend. Then Big John, who could without sound run down and catch a wild rabbit, began to run as he had not run for years, and after a time the heavy pursuing footsteps were left far behind. He felt that Manitou was with him, keeping the Child silent, so he plunged off the trail, directly into the thick, screening forest. It did not matter now if a twig snapped under his feet. There was no one to hear.

Olafson came running back to the cabin, red of face from his efforts and intensely angry. Willyum was sitting on the cabin step, planing a board leisurely, smoothly, quietly, as though time and the affairs of other men were non-existent, but he was relieved and delighted when he saw that the running man was alone and Big John had somehow outwitted him. He looked up incuriously as the foreigner hurried toward him, calling as he came," Where'd she go?" "Who are you wanting?" questioned Willyum, placidly and maddeningly ignorant. "That hellish little biting wildcat. She ran this way. When I get my hands of her, again, I'll ---" He held up his hand and blood was running from it."I do not see him, me," interrupted Willyum unconcernedly and his eyes were deliberately vague and his mouth was smiling affably. "And that is only small cut on big man. "Where's that big Indian fellow that was here with you a while ago?" asked Olafson savagely. "Which way did he go? Maybe he seen the kid." "That Big John you are wanting? Oh, she go home long time ago, soon after you go wit' those Deneece-Freedah. Her house is down the odder trail, and I don' see her going, me." Willyum's eyes were only mildly interested as the foreigner looked searchingly at him.

"Seems mighty damned funny to me, how she could disappear almost in front of my eyes. Can you get some fellows together right away to help me hunt for her? I don't know your woods very well," said Olafson. "Surest thing. We don' want losing those Deneece-Freedah, us," assured Willyum, though he marked the "very well" in his memory to tell Big John. He left his work at the coffin. Then he closed the cabin door until Kahnee should come later, and without haste turned toward Olafson and nodded an invitation to come along.

The outlander followed him into many Indian houses on the trail, eyeing him with suspicion every minute, while they enlisted probably a dozen willing men in the search party.

For three days they searched the vicinity where the Child had been lost, and also other parts of the Island to which she might possibly have wandered, but she had mysteriously disappeared. Big John and all the other Indians who were asked to help were interested and gave their best efforts. They walked the foreigner from one end of the long Island to the other, in zigzags, until he was almost too weary to stand. The keenest trackers worked with him steadily from dawn-light to dark, but not one small footprint of the Child could they discover. Mr. Vargatte, who was helping on the second day, suavely suggested to Olafson that they should get the sheriff down from town to assist them, and was amused when the outlander became angry and abruptly dismissed Theophile's idea. The Frenchman smiled directly into the cold eyes of Olafson and urbanely commented that the Islanders also hated outside interference with their family affairs, and for once the stranger's eyes dropped before those of another man.

However, the search went on, because Olafson was grim and determined. They went into every Indian house on the Island which might be a possible hiding place, and searched it thoroughly, none of the owners objecting when Big John explained lengthily that they were hunting for the Child. They beat the woods, in ever-widening circles, without finding a trace of her, or sign of her passing. No one could suggest where she might be, or seemed to have an opinion. Olafson's trick of suddenly and unexpectedly appearing at a lonely cabin in the woods where she might be hidden, brought no results. Finally he began to think the Indians were telling the truth when they declared they knew nothing about the Child. For the first time in his experience he was meeting a secretive, inscrutable race which could be as hard and cruel as he was, if necessary, and much more subtle than he could comprehend. He could not believe that a people which he considered half-civilized would care too-greatly what happened to any child. What was one half-wit more or-less anyhow! Even a beautiful one was not worth so much trouble and effort. She might possibly have fallen into the bog which was so close to the trail where she had been lost, as Big John explained, and been drowned without a sound being heard by anyone. Many things might have happened to a child, desperate and lost in the thick green timber of so large an Island. They told him ghastly tales of other strayed children who had never been found. His search became more and more spasmodic, and he spent more of his time in the Indian cabins, especially those in which there were pretty Indian girls. They made him blandly welcome, with hard eyes and smiling mouths, and detained him with all the wiles at their disposal. And always a man remained in the cabin, smiling also, but watching, and Olafson understood. It became a game with him which he never won, but all the more fascinating because he did not.

While Big John and most of the men were helping Olafson search for the Child, Kahnee, Celestina, Telesphore and Madeline planned for the burial of the Strange Woman. Big John was never home except at night and was then so silent they hesitated to disturb him. Telesphore was thoroughly irate, and would have ignored or disputed hotly any authority of Olafson in the matter, but the foreigner was absolutely indifferent as to what happened to the Woman. The Child was his interest; they could dispose of the mother as they chose. Madeline grieved that only after her death they had learned anything about her. The women clothed her in a white dress contributed by Madame Delongue, and Telesphore made a simple cross to mark the grave, and carved upon it her real name. Under this he cut their own name for her: HILDA -- THE STRANGE WOMAN.

They had asked permission from a bemused Big John to bury her on the Indian mound as if she were one of their tribe and he assented gladly. So the morning after the Child had disappeared, in the early dawn they carried the Strange Woman through the woods and laboriously climbed the steep, awkward steps re-cut in the slope of the clay mound. Madeline had never been there before, and as they brought the Strange Woman to the place Willyum had prepared for her, close to a tall, drooping elm, Madeline, startled by its sunny openness in contrast to the deep shade of the woods-path from which they had come, clung to Telesphore's hand and wished with all her heart that they might have as beautiful a place in which to rest. As Telesphore read the last prayer, dramatically yet sincerely solemn and reverent, she looked far across the green-blue lake and into the purple Canadian hills. She was glad the Strange Woman would always be so close to Jennie and Waubegoon, in this secret place. On its wind-cooled summit a mourner's grief would be eased and he would gradually come to know the intimacy of star-shine, the sun-spun leaves, cob-webbed morning dew, the soft little noises carried on the night wind, and timid deer feeding in the moonlight. She loved the beauty and silence of it more than did

Kahnee, who accepted its strange loveliness with the placidity of long usage and familiarity.

When they had finished their task and the small white cross was firmly in place, they lingered for a time, looking at the scene spread out below them and listening to the bird songs. As they stood there, they became aware that on the same side of the huge mound sat an Indian woman, close beside a small, new grave, her head bent low in mourning, her hot, feverish eyes staring at the tiny heap of earth which covered her beloved child. Then, above the faint whirring of the decorative scarlet pinwheels and many-colored paper streamers rustling in the breeze, she heard the spontaneous lament of the bereaved mother for her baby, buried only a few hours before they had arrived on the mound. Madeline had grown to understand the depth of the Indian woman's undemonstrative love for her children, but there was revealed to her in this woman's own grief-song a poignant hurt and longing that transcended any sorrow she had ever heard a white woman express. Involuntarily they listened as her reiterated chant of pain and woe was carried to them by the wind.

>"Aih-ah! Great Spirit!
> At the End's Edge
>Where we step over into Blackness,
>Blackness deeper than man has ever seen,
>Thick and unfathomable Blackness,
>Lonely beyond all human knowledge,
>My too-small child stands
>Waiting, at the End's Edge.
>
>He has but now stepped over
>Into that Vast Darkness,
>That Mystic darkness of death,
>Teeming with wicked spirits.
>
>Aih-ah! Great Spirit!
>Shorten my life.
> Let me also step
>Over the End's Edge,
>That I may hold close
>His small shaking hand

And lead him through the great,
Evil Blackness.
He is too small to go alone."

As Madeline listened, her mood changed, and she saw behind the wild grandeur of the place some of the sadness Jennie had felt so bitterly and had tried to make her understand. She realized the hard reality so close underneath the natural beauty, and felt she could not bear the sudden burden of grief for the hopeless mother which had come upon her. If she had tried only a little harder to understand Jennie's complaint, and help her, she might not now have felt such a sense of guilt. "Take me home, now, Telesphore," she begged him. "I cannot bear to see anyone so hurt, so broken."

Telesphore tried to reassure her, attempted to explain that death was no harder to endure on the Island than in the city, but Madeline was too sorrow-stricken to listen. So he took her hand in his and they walked side by side, as Theophile and Delima had done years before, down the path to the Settlement and the commonplace acts of living again. Kahnee and Celestina followed more slowly, and though Celestina understood some of Madeline's feeling, Kahnee was at peace, and deeply thankful that her loved ones could rest unmolested by the curiosity of unwanted strangers.

When the women returned to the Big John cabin, they found him at home and quite cheerful for he believed that Olafson was losing interest in his search and would soon leave the Island. Though the girls were skeptical, Big John was right. At the end of the week, Big John took the time to make a special trip to town in his motor boat, and watched from the depot waiting room while Olafson boarded the train going south. He returned to the Island, grinning with relief and gladness, and was more contented and really happy than they had seen him since Jennie's death. The Indians were wary, however. Big John waited an entire week after Olafson had gone, fearing he might plan to surprise them by an unexpected visit. Then Theophile Vargatte assured Big John that the foreigner would never bother them again. They both laughed heartily, as at a good joke, and Theophile congratulated Big John on his wisdom in avoiding outside intervention from the law by playing up to Olafson.

When Big John left the store, he went for a long tramp to some mysterious destination which he refused to disclose, even to his wife. When he returned he was carrying the Child in his arms. He stood her in the middle of the big living room beside Mrs. Big John's rocker, and Mrs. Big John carefully and with exceeding tenderness unwrapped the warm shawl from around the Child. The family group was watching eagerly. At the sight of the kind brown faces, which she had always known, the Child laughed with delight, and held tightly to the ministering fingers of Jane Big John. The family came closer, all toward the center of the room. Softly and possessively they touched the golden ringlets and smoothed the wrinkled dress, patting her with reassuring little touches all the while. But the Child had forgotten that she had ever been frightened or hurt, and gurgled at all of them. They glowed at her response and happily believed that she recognized them. She was theirs, with all her empty, lovely laughter and joyousness. Twice the Great Spirit had given her to them in strange fashion. All except Kahnee were filled with a deep content and a sense of safety, for at last they were sure they would have her with them always. Kahnee rejoiced with them that the Child was home, but she pondered a question which had worried her all summer. Celestina was glad only because she loved the Child and wanted her with them.

Mrs. Big John held out her arms to Deneece. "Come, dear small-one," she coaxed. "My arms have ached to hold you again." As if she understood what Mrs. Big John asked, the Child climbed willingly upon her lap and snuggled her head down on the old woman's shoulder. Mrs. Big John smiled at the others and began to rock the Child, with an infinite peace which had not been hers since she had learned that Waubegoon's baby had gone from the Island with Bill Crash and his mother. As she swayed back and forth, she crooned the old lullaby of her own mother over and over, the Child closed her eyes, and finally slept. As the plaintive humming became more drowsy and faint, the others tip-toed about their evening tasks. Again the Child had brought gladness with her into their house, and perhaps this time it would remain.

CHAPTER XIII
KAHNEE

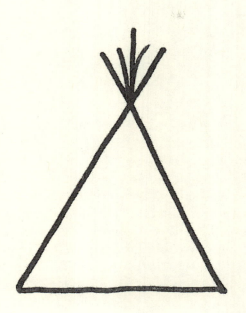

**SYMBOL OF THE DOMESTIC CIRCLE,
OR A HOMEMAKER**

KAHNEE

Much to the delight of the Big John family, Telesphore and Madeline decide to live one whole year on the Island. They enjoy the average, carefree life of the Island population of French and Indians. They also become very fond of the Child who is growing into a strikingly beautiful girl. They keep the Child at their cabin as much as possible, and notice her natural friendship with animals and birds, which seem absolutely unafraid of her.

Telesphore frankly warns the Indians of what may happen if some wandering, unscrupulous hunter should perchance meet the Child while she is roaming alone in the woods. All this has no effect on Big John. Despite his experience with the Child's own father, he stubbornly insists that the Child will be safe with them, and that she must be allowed to do as she pleases, with no restraint of her liberty.

Madeline and Kahnee hunt for the Child one evening, when they suddenly become aware that she is too long gone. They discover her in company with a stranger, who seems to be trying to entice her farther and farther away. They call the Child, and the stranger goes off into the woods. They do not know if he had intended to harm the Child or had been trying to talk with her. As the Child comes toward them in answer to their summons, a will-of-the-wisp floats out from a swamp close by and floats behind and after the Child.

[Author's note to this paragraph: This Kahnee will tell Madeline.] The significance of the appearance of the will-of-the-wisp close to the Child, and apparently following her, is one of evil to come. A malevolent spirit takes the form of this light and, thus disguised, can wreak vengeance or malice upon its unsuspecting victim. It can creep through the smallest crack below a window or door, and steal a man's soul away from him as he sleeps. If it does not choose to return the soul, the next day the man walks about without one, or as long as the will-of-the-wisp wishes to keep it. Any Indian chooses death in preference to being without a soul, which they do seem to connect with mind. After the will-of-the-wisp has once shown that it has designs upon any certain person, that person must be removed from the locality, for his own safety.

Kahnee's unselfish love for the Child makes her decide that she must over-step her privileges and by argument and coercion force Big John to send the Child to a safer place. Only the will-of-the-wisp and its evil intention could make her do this thing, which is beyond the common privileges of any Indian woman. She finally forces Big John to admit she is right and the Child must go.

CHAPTER XIV
KABBAISHE

**KABABISHE, THE SCREECH OWL
SYMBOL OF EVIL OR MISFORTUNE**

KABABISHE (SCREECH OWL)

Mr. Vargatte and his wife come to tell the Big John family that he has sold the store, because of his wife's poor health. Vargatte also tells Big John, as gently as he can, that Big John has lost the mail route, which he has had for many years. He is too old now to work for the "government." Abe is to remain with the new storekeeper, and Vargatte will not be leaving until the new man comes and gets settled. Madame Vargatte will go sooner, to get the new house in the city ready, and also to take the Child to an institution. Vargatte has already made the arrangements for this. Their visit and their sad news are foreshadowed for Big John by the call of a screech owl which has been staying about their cabin. The voice of Kababishe, the screech owl, is supposed by the Indians to foretell misfortune or death.

[Author's note to this chapter: "Very briefly----"]

CHAPTER XV
THE LAST OMEN

SYMBOL OF DEATH

THE LAST OMEN

Big John sat in his favorite place on the front stoop, staring into space and brooding, a habit which had seemed to grow upon him increasingly. The afternoon was more than half gone, and Kahnee looked at him with wistful curiosity as she passed him on her way into the living room, her arms full of clean, white basket-stripe to put into the dye-kettle. Since he had learned from Theophile Vargatte that he had lost the mail-route, he had not acted naturally with any of them, not even Jane Big John, who was usually his first consideration. The family did not question him, nor did they comment even among themselves on his strange behavior, for he was the head of the tribe and what he might choose to do or say was not to be questioned by any of them. But they often wondered what he was thinking as he sat gazing out across the blue lake, seeing nothing, not hearing them when they spoke to him.

However, most of the time Big John was not aware that they were wondering about him, or that he had changed in any way. This habit of self-analysis was a new thing to him, and he did not realize how far it was carrying him mentally from them all. Never before had he questioned the rightness or merit of his own actions; nor had he ever asked himself if a better result might have happened if he had acted differently. He had followed the old traditions and habits of his people, and accepted the consequences as a matter of course. He was never at peace with himself since this habit of wondering had gripped him. The bitter self-blame which came into his mind when he thought of Jennie and realized that together they might have worked out a solution to her troubles made him unsure of his wisdom, which until now he had, naively, never doubted. The uncertainty troubled him, but, habitually, most of all he was worried about Joe Pete.

After one short letter to Big John at the time of Jennie's death, there had been no direct word from Joe Pete, and Big John, though he said nothing of it to his family, and hoped they did not know, grieved deeply in secret at the boy's apparent neglect of their desires and plans for him. They had sent Joe Pete out into the white man's world with great expectations that he would return to the Island and pass what he had learned on to the tribe, to help them to grow and prosper. He was the chosen one of the Ojibways; in Big John's estimation a thoroughbred Indian with not one drop of alien blood in him. Under the trials he had endured on the Island he had stood firm, and had done the honest thing always. They had watched him and waited, aloof and unhelping, testing him, to be certain that he was the right child to send. As he sat on his porch this gay, late-spring afternoon, Big John was forced to ask himself whether they had shown wisdom in their choice. What had happened to Joe Pete in the great outside world, where he lived a different life in a strange environment, and faced many other kinds of temptation than he had known and resisted in the isolated clearing where he had lived on the Island! Was it perhaps the affection for his small, blind brother which had held him steadfast, or was it an inherent quality of real greatness! After all, the boy had not had much choice of action on the Island. When would they know the answer to all his questions. They had no money for extra expenses, so Joe Pete had never returned to the Island after he had once departed from it. He had never promised to fulfill any of their plans and they had never asked a pledge of him to return. They had simply trusted that he would. Now he was about to graduate from another, bigger Indian School than the state one to which he had been first sent. The white men in these schools had been kind to the boy, and had constantly pushed him on and into situations which would develop a sense of responsibility in him. They all knew what Big John wanted of them and were glad to cooperate with him. Very soon it would be the date when the annual letter from the superintendent of the Indian school would arrive, and Big John was anxious to know what he would write. The closeness of the arrival of the letter had excited and bothered him. Theophile Vargatte was as interested as Big John, but his mind was completely filled with the problem of selling out his goods to his successor, and his final preparations to leave the Island, and he could not find the time for their old, long talks. Why had Joe Pete never added a word to the letters from the superintendent and say what he intended doing!

However, as he pondered, staring into the blue horizon of the lake, Big John's thoughts became more cheerful. It might even be that they were planning a surprise as Mr. Brand and Jennie had done, so long ago it seemed now to Big John. Probably Joe Pete would simply walk in upon them some day without announcing his arrival beforehand, and would not leave them again. Why should he announce himself? He was one of the tribe and it would be the natural and right thing for him to come to his home when he was ready. He belonged there on the Island, and would certainly return again to his own place. He and Jim would work well together, and together they would achieve the goals which Big John had long ago planned for the younger generation of his tribe. He could visualize the new cabins they would build in place of the old huts; more schools would be provided, closer to far-flung homes; the roads would be kept open all winter; the younger people would be more closely knit as a group; there was no end to the things these two young men would do. Joe Pete would be the planner and the go-between for the Indians in their contacts with the whites; Jim would carry out the plans, for, though he lacked the creative mind, he had the gift of an easy ability to get along harmoniously with people and have them work willingly with him. Thus Big John consoled himself, and Kahnee was glad to see that his face had smoothed out its worry-lines when she went out again for another bundle of basket timber. School would be dismissed in June. Tomorrow or the next day they would hear definitely. Either Joe Pete would write or return. How good it would be to have the boy home again! They could get together at the old hunting lodge which Jerry had given him, and repair it so that Joe Pete could live in it very comfortably. Big John forced himself to think of that hunting lodge without Jennie in it, and change the plans they had made years ago, that it should be theirs when they both returned to the Island, wise with knowledge and trained in the ways of the whites. He filled the lodge with images of Joe Pete planning and working, and if a misty, discontented girl-ghost hovered about the edges of his dreams, he refused to acknowledge her. Surely Manitou would not deny him the fulfillment of this, his last plan!

His mind was still wandering in his air-castles when Celestina came from the store with the groceries and brought the letter for which he had been waiting. He held it in his hands a long time, and wished Theophile Vargatte could read it to him and then they could talk it over together and make plans. Theophile would laugh as he read, and his eyes would sparkle and tease as he talked. Big John sighed, then asked Celestina to read the letter to them all, glad that she could do it so fluently, and rose from the stoop and accompanied the black-eyed girl to the living room, where the others were gathered. There they were all talking before the supper hour. Celestina knew what hopes Big John had placed in this letter from Joe Pete, and all the way home had loitered, dreading this honor of reading that Big John had given her since she came to live with them. She was also assailed by doubts. If Joe Pete had decided to return, why should there be a letter! She could see that this thought had not come to the others, whose reactions and conclusions were slower than hers. She looked around the small circle of faces, now become so dear to her, and caught Jim's reassuring nod. The late afternoon sun was yellowing the cabin's big room, so she sat where the sun glowed brightest and opened the envelope. She glanced over its contents hastily, and a shivering fear took possession of her. She tried to speak, but her lips trembled and she could not form the words she had to read. Her heart was filled with a deep love for Big John, which had grown so understanding that she forgot and forgave the faults which had tantalized her when she first came to their cabin. At her hesitation they all glanced toward her, but politely, sidewise. She looked again to Jim for encouragement. "Must I read it?" she almost pleaded of him.

At her question they surmised what the letter said, but Jim nodded. "Yes, my Celestina. You know Kahnee and I cannot read. There is no one else except an outsider, and him we do not want. We must know what the letter says."

Celestina read slowly, for the sorrow she was feeling for Big John made her throat thick and aching. As was usual with the Indian, Joe Pete told his plans in the fewest words, without any softening of the blow he knew they would inflict. Even Celestina's sympathetic voice, stumbling through the reading, could not alleviate the hurt that was coming to Big John.

Dear Big John,

I am never coming to the Island again. The superintenddent wants me to come up there and see you and talk about it all before I make a decision, but what is the use to talk a thing which is already decided by things we cannot change? On the Island there is not much good land, and we have not the machinery to cultivate it. And where would we Indians ever get the money to buy machines, and the good land, and fix the cabins so they would be fit to live in, as the whites live? Certainly not from the basket money the women make! Now that Jennie is dead, I have made up my mind that I will not come back to the place. Kahnee and Moses can have that old cabin Jerry gave me. I do not want it. I am going to the big towns where the other boys tell me is much good work and fun and easy money.

They do not like it here in the school that I am not coming back to you, and they say I owe you much, but that is not their business for I am not a child any more to be told what I must do or what I must not do. When I have worked for a time I will send some money to you and Mr. Vargatte what you have spent for me. I wish for you that you are all well.

       Yours truly,
          Joseph Peter Shingoos

When Celestina at last finished reading she was weeping without being aware of her tears, but with bitterness flooding her. Her cheeks were red with anger. "That is a cruel, ugly letter," she cried indignantly. "I have never seen this boy, Joe Pete, but I will always hate him for this bad, wicked thing he has written to our father Big John. Like a stranger he signs a letter to those who have loved and cared for him, 'yours truly'! I think he is -------"

Jim held up his hand significantly and she became quiet. "That is not a thing for you to say, Celestina," he rebuked her gently. "This affair rests only with my father and with Joe Pete. And, after all, what person has the right to say which trail his friend or his enemy shall walk! That, each must choose for himself. All our tribe believe this to be true, and no one must deny a man his born privilege."

He looked toward his father for confirmation of this, one of the strongest tenets of their creed of living, and was appalled at the expression of pain and disappointment obvious to all in Big John's face. This decision of a boy not of their family was a keener hurt to the big Indian than the deaths of his daughters or the departure of the Child had been. Greatly as he had loved Waubegoon and Jennie, when they had died he had been consoled and heartened, without their realizing the fact, by the idea that this boy they had sent to the big Indian school would carry on. Jim could only stare unbelievingly at his father, and wonder at the affection and ambitions he had centered in this lad who was not his son, and suddenly knew a wicked jealousy and hatred of Joe Pete. He had not until this moment suspected the strength of Big John's feeling that another boy possessed superiority of mind and aspiration over that of his own sons. He asked himself why his father did not recognize and acknowledge his own and Young John's quickness of perception of the difficulties of the tribe, and their problems, and their attempts to solve some of them. He had always felt he would be willing to work with Joe Pete when he returned to the Island, but he had understood they were to work as equals, not with the one a leader and himself a follower. He looked at Celestina with an awakened understanding and solicitude in his eyes, and at the same moment caught Kahnee's swift glance of warning. She was concerned only for their father and the effect this letter would have upon him, and their own reactions would have to wait for further discussion when they were alone. Instantly his hatred and envy passed as quickly as they had come to him, and he wondered what Big John would say to them in this time of disillusionment. As he waited for his father to speak, a queer sensation of uncertainty came over him, and again he was a small boy listening for his father to pass judgment on some misbehavior.

But Big John remained silent, for he could not say a word to them which would explain how he felt. He had again the same sick nausea which he had experienced on the night he had walked alone on the trail after leaving Waubegoon with Bill Crash. He wondered dully how often this sensation of illness would overpower him when he really should be feeling anger or resentment. His mind seemed deadened, incapable of stirring with any kind of emotion. He did not want to look at his family, though he knew Jim was expecting him to answer Celestina. He was ashamed of this numbness which lay so heavily upon him that his wonted unquenchable spirit could not flash through.

Though Kahnee was aching with distress and a feeling of desolation, she showed none of it. Pretending that she was going to the store-shed for more sweet-grass, she crossed the room. She placed her big, awkward-looking hand upon her father's shoulder as she passed him, and he patted it uncertainly. Jim wondered why

Kahnee felt ashamed of hands that had done so much for her family. When she opened the door, the orange light of evening filled the room, and a "sun-going-down" wind stirred the litter of gay basket strips on the floor and fluttered the strings of herbs which hung from the ceiling. As the herbs swayed, almost imperceptibly, something soft and shadowy dropped from the beams and fell upon Big John's hand. He started as the thing touched him and then clung to his fingers. Involuntarily he shook his hand, but the object was not dislodged. Celestina ran to him. "What is it, father Big John? What is it?"

Big John rose quickly and held his hand to the light which streamed into the room through the door opened by Kahnee. Clinging tenaciously to them still, and dripping its torn filaments from his fingers, they all saw an enormous cobweb, dark gray and heavy with the dust of the winter housework and fires. Horrified, they jumped to their feet. Mrs. Big John clung so tightly to the arms of her old rocker that her brown knuckles became white with the strain. And at that moment there was wafted into the room a peculiar, evil, uncanny odor, the essence of decay and death. Big John rubbed his hands together, almost aimlessly, but seemingly could not rid himself of the sticky web. The family stood aghast and unmoving, watching every movement he made. Celestina stared at them all in amazement. "Oh, what is it, Jim! What has come to our father! Ka-ah-nee, what is the matter with everybody! Tell me!"

As though her frantic exclamations had awakened him from a stupor of fear, Big John answered her. "It is a sign. I cannot rid my hands of the sign. And it is the odor of death, which has crept into the room. The Black Shadow hovers ever nearer to our house!"

"No, it doesn't," contradicted Celestina decidedly. "It isn't! It is only a big dirty cobweb which has dropped from the ceiling, and which Ka-ah-nee or I should have long ago swept down. See, my father. I can wipe it from your hands with my own, easily. It is sticky because it is old and full of dust. And that smell is only from that great, queer-spotted toadstool which grows so close to the stoop that I smell it every time I go near the door. I have been asking Ka-ah-nee what kind it is for a day or so. Now it is older and rotten, and the smell becomes worse. It comes with the night-wind into the room."

"Be quiet, Celestina," commanded Jim, seeming to her as emotionless as usual. "You do not understand this thing. You cannot overcome an omen with woman-talk. My father knows the old signs and reads into them the things we younger ones do not know. What he speaks is always the truth, for he knows, as did all his fathers before him."

Kahnee nodded agreement as Celestina stared at them in bewilderment at their unquestioning acceptance of an idea which was to her incomprehensible.

"There have been many signs that I shall not be an old helpless man in this my house," said Big John softly, almost inaudibly, as if reassuring himself of something he had always known. "But again I say, with Jim, something you must always remember. Each one must choose his own path, and ever thereafter walk upon it without flinching. Even those who are closest to a man cannot keep him from feeling alone. And Jim, you and our Young John must go on as we planned. Our family is small now, but closely woven together, and in that is your strength. They will have willingness to help. Now I shall go and tell our friend, Theophile Vargatte, what the letter said. He must know."

They watched him, through the open door, until he reached the old oak at the turn of the trail. There he hesitated, turned toward them, and for a moment lifted his hand fumblingly in his customary farewell gesture. As he vanished from sight, Jim turned and was amazed to see tears dropping upon Kahnee's hands as she bent, weaving gay colors in the basket which must be finished before morning.

CHAPTER XIV
BIG JOHN

**SYMBOL OF THE DEATH OF A MAN
WHOSE TOTEM IS THE EAGLE**

BIG JOHN

During the first three weeks in January the Islanders did not once see the sun. Snow fell steadily, constantly, until their entire small world was filled with the softly dropping flakes. The little cabins put on strange and grotesque snow-berets, fences were covered from sight, trails were obliterated as if they had never existed, and a man on snowshoes sank at every step deep into the downy, yielding mass. Color was wiped from the landscape and dead, monotonous feather-white took its place, except where cold blue shadows lay. The Big Johns were shut in at their end of the unused trail, and from their windows they could not see even the nearest trees. Jim forced his way through the great drifts to the store twice, but was weary to illness when he returned with the needed groceries, which he pulled behind him on the toboggan, leaving in the snow a foot-deep trail. Sled runners could not have come through.

The dead quiet of the snow-muffled woods had entered their cabin. No one spoke unless it was necessary. Big John had allowed his bitterness of mind to accumulate until he was overwhelmed with it. He sat near the stove, brooding over his unwonted uselessness and spoke to none of them, even in reply to a direct question. They understood, and cherished no resentment toward him. Mrs. Big John sat quietly through his silence, seemingly unworried, but secretly and constantly watching him through half-closed lids. Kahnee stolidly went on with her weaving, matching her colors as painstakingly as though nothing unusual were oppressing the cabin with this great weight of stillness, which none of them could throw off. The longer it remained unbroken, the greater was the task of speaking, never easy for these reserved people. Every morning they awoke hopefully, looking quickly to see if the sun were shining through the thick-frosted panes, and each day they again saw only a dusky light and more snowflakes. Celestina, who could not be so stoical as the others, became weary of the white world without and the lifelessness within. She thought that if the clumps of snow could only be blown by a wild storm in some other direction than straight down, endlessly dripping from an opaque gray sky, she could better endure being caged in a little cabin. But when the wind arose as if in answer to her wish, moaning like the first inharmonic tuning-up of a giant orchestra, and blowing the snow in whirling masses, she hated it more than the silence. When the wind struck a shrill, wild note as it met the clothesline strung across the open front porch, she felt she must put her fingers in her ears to shut out the sound. Jim looked out into the gloom and was glad Moses and Young John were in the camps with other men, and rather envied their drawing their pay while they waited for the snow to settle enough so they might get into the deep timber and at their work. While they waited they were probably listening to wild yarns from other lumberjacks and laughing together at wilder jokes. Food would be plentiful, and the stoves red-hot, fighting against this bitter cold which seeped through every unchinked crack in the walls and around the windows.

Then one morning the silence was broken. The younger ones were awakened by an unusual sound, and when they came downstairs they saw Big John sitting by the window, still gazing emptily at his big hands, grown flabby from idleness, and he was racked with coughing. His wife had stumbled about, trying to find remedies in the house which would help, but nothing has stopped the spasm. She had not wanted to waken them, for they could do no more for their father than she could. Even the mixtures which the Very Oldest Mother had compounded from herbs, gathered from their own woods, failed to relieve him. He had been awake all night, and a peculiar bluish tint had overlaid the satin-brown of his face.

"That is what comes then from getting wet while he carried in some wood yesterday," said Celestina regretfully and Kahnee nodded. "The Old Ones should let those younger do the hard work for them," continued Celestina, "and Jim would have been glad ----"

But now Kahnee disagreed with her. "My father is not so old then, him," she contradicted, too flatly, because she was more worried than she would admit, and hated to have Celestina say openly what they were all thinking. For the first time, at Celestina's words, the thought came to her that possibly her father might be older than they realized. Somehow the idea filled her with a sick terror which she fought against but could not get out of her mind.

Older people could not fight an illness with the strength of youth. They had all leaned upon their father so long; not only his own family but the whole tribe were dependent upon his advice and wisdom. He had always been too courteous, too gentle with their faults and blunders and they had all probably overburdened him with their petty problems. Now they must begin to ease him by bearing their own troubles or finding solutions to them. They were children no longer. Looking back over the years, Kahnee could see that her father had not seemed free of worry since Waubegoon had gone from them.

Though Big John declared petulantly that he felt better and coughed less when he was sitting in the big rocker; toward evening they coaxed him to go to bed and remain there. Gusts of keenly cold wind came into the house under the doors and loosely fitted window sills, and they were afraid he would become chilled. Jim sent his mother to bed and sat with his father during the night. The spells of coughing came ever more frequently, and Jim had to support him in a sitting position while they lasted. Big John began to have difficulty in breathing, and the boy propped him high in bed with pillows. The hours seemed endless to Jim, who had never before seen anyone so ill. Many sober, deep thoughts passed through his mind that night. Sitting there in the dim firelight, and planning for the future, he came into full manhood.

During the next day they realized that Big John grew steadily worse. They could see him becoming weaker while they sat watching him, helpless to relieve him in any way. Every time his father coughed and weakly complained of the great, tearing pain in his chest, Jim would vow he was going up to the town and bring a doctor back to the cabin. He paced the floor impatiently, hating all at once their isolation and the beating, blinding storm. He knew he could not get through to the Crossing, and no boat could possibly take him over the lake in such a storm. From the mainland they could not even see him through this curtain of falling snow, and would not know he was there, waiting to cross. The Indians further up in the Narrows would have their boats hauled high on the banks and put away for the winter. They would be buried under the drifts, and it was useless to expect help there. The ice, which had formed during the week of bitter weather, had been broken by the gale, and he would not dare to try their usual winter travel on it. The family waited, uncomplaining and as stoically as they could, hoping the snow would stop and give Jim, and through him Big John, a chance.

Toward evening, Theophile Vargatte broke through the woods-trail from his store to the cabin on snowshoes. He came in, winded and panting, shaking whiteness from his shoulders and cap, stamping chunks of it from his high boots, and thundering maledictions on the ever-so-accursed weather that kept friends from seeing each other for weeks at a time. To the welcoming group, he seemed as strong and rugged as the rock-blue Canadian hills which were their horizon when he entered, laughing and greeting each one specially and familiarly between grunts and complaints. When he saw Big John lying so whitely silent on the bed in the corner of the hot room, and realized he was seriously ill, his laughter was shut off immediately. When Jim had told him in the store that Big John was sick, he had thought the boy was scared and had exaggerated the situation.

"Now tell me how it goes," he urged them.

Jim answered, quietly so he would not disturb his father. "I think he is more tired and discouraged than sick in his body," he tried to explain. "He is overburdened and weary in his mind from the many hard things which have happened to him. It is as if he has been hurt by much beating with a stick." He hesitated, groping for words which would make clear to the Frenchman what he meant. "Not in his body, but in his mind. His body would get better if his mind could be freed of its misery."

Theophile Vargatte looked at the boy and nodded. He understood what Jim was trying to explain. Then he went close to the bed and looked down on the big Indian he had known so intimately for many years. They had not always been in accord in their points of view, but they were both big men and had always been fair and honest with each other. Each had respected the other's racial difference from himself in all its phases, and their friendship had grown deep and sincere. Surely Big John could not be so ill as he seemed, if the boy were right; Theophile's eyes were cloudy with tears.

"Big John! My old friend Big John! And are you then so ill that you must remain in the bed!" his voice was pitiful as he called to his big friend for recognition. Theophile was never ashamed to betray his emotions. But Big John did not know him, though his eyes flickered open and stared intently up at him. Then again Big

John coughed, and when Theophile placed his hand on Big John's forehead, even in his inexperience he knew his old friend was too hot with fever. The big Indian held his shaking hands close to his face and muttered something, this time loud enough so Vargatte could hear the slurred words. But Big John spoke in Ojibway, and these were words Theophile had never heard before. He looked at Jim and the boy reluctantly translated what his father had said.

"He says, 'The evil odor of Death is on my hands and in my nostrils. It is like a cloud over my bed, and covers me like a raven's black wing.' He has been saying that all the afternoon, and he has been talking about walking lonesomely through a dark trail to find Waubegoon. We believe he is again living that night when he followed our sister to bring her back to our mother and he came alone, him. Too many bad things have come to our father, and he is weak with hopelessness. And since he lost the mail-run he has not been like himself."

"I know, I know, me," Theophile agreed. "But, Jim, would not he breathe easier if you opened the door at times and let the cooler air into the room? I have been told that those who are sick like Big John is, breathe better in the fresh air. And are you going after a doctor when you can travel? He should have help which we cannot give him."

Jim shrugged his shoulders wearily, in that inimitable gesture of the Indian. He had hoped that Monsieur Vargatte would offer some suggestions, or plan some method of getting help for Big John. Now he discovered, to his complete amazement, that Theophile was as helpless as they, and had nothing to offer. He had no more power in a crisis than had the Indians. Jim looked at him as if he were staring at a stranger who had come into their home. His childish ideas of the power of this Frenchman, and all whites, dropped from him. But as he gazed, he felt again all the charm, the honest friendliness of Vargatte, and realized anew his real affection and loyalty for Big John. His own old warmth of feeling for Theophile came back. The Frenchman was looking directly at him and speaking. While he had been following his strange line of thought he had lost some of what had been said. "-----and tell the doctor that he shall be paid for any service he can render to my old friend. You may not have enough money ready in the house, my Jim. Come to the store as soon as you can get out, and we shall speedily arrange matters. And when you get to town, perhaps then you should speak to Father Lalliere [*to see if he could come and administer Last Rights, if it comes to that."*

Jim was distraught —what]* would they do without Big John! His kindness! His wisdom! He looked at his mother, at Celestina, at Kahnee, thought of the absent Young John, and decided that he would accept fully his father's responsibility toward them all. Firm lines of adult determination came into his face as he made his decision. Kahnee glanced at him occasionally, wondered what he was thinking, and thought how much he looked like Big John. They were so deeply engrossed in their own meditations, they did not notice that when the gray dawn-light crept through the windows, Big John opened his eyes and looked at them all. He was conscious again. His voice was rasping as he said with difficulty, "The wind has stopped."

Jim glanced swiftly from the window. "So also has the snowing," he answered quietly. "Now I shall start out for the town to get the doctor, even though you are better."

Big John looked at them as if he could never see enough of them. Slowly, every word dragging and scraping as it left his throat, he said, conserving each sound. "No doctor, my Jim. I am no better, but a doctor cannot help me. Bring Father Lalliere to me soon."

Dumbly they sat, uncomprehending and shocked at what they had heard. Big John would not ask Father Lalliere to make such a trip unless he were in the last extremity of illness and knew it. Celestina sobbed. Jim licked his dry lips and coaxed Big John. "The doctor too, my father? They can make strong magic over the sick. Let him try!"

Big John closed his eyes and lay still, as if he were drawing strength from some secret inner depth. "No --only the priest. Pay'-kinah-gay, our helper, --our kind one. I need him. Go quickly, for I cannot -- wait -- much --- longer."

Celestina felt that she could not bear their silent acceptance of Big John's words. She cried wildly, "But father Big John! The snow is deep, deeper than you know, and Jim may not be able to bring the priest through the drifts. They are higher than the roof and too soft. And Father Lalliere is old and worn, and weak. The city doctor is strong. He can follow in Jim's trail and, come to make you well again."

**A page of the manuscript is missing; text in italics added by Editor.*

Big John did not seem to hear. He gazed at Jim, and his great affection for his son was plain in his eyes. His voice became stronger, more urgent.

"Go, Jim. Father Lalliere --the Winner-- will come. Never in fifty years has he failed when we needed him. He will come." His words faded into soundlessness.

"What shall I tell Father Lalliere?" Jim asked of them. But Big John answered. Even in his last weakness he was still the chief of the clan; demanding obedience from them, and there was something prophetic in the tones of his voice which took them back in memory to the day when the Very Oldest Woman had assumed command of the crowd after Waubegoon's death. Celestina crossed herself.

"Say to him that his old friend Big John is walking the Black Trail. Much trouble has come to me. My pack is too heavy . Tomorrow I die. Go now, my Jim. Make no more talk. I do not know -- how far ---- into tomorrow -- I can wait."

Arguing no longer, Jim bundled into his warmest coat. Celestina wrapped the woolen scarf about his neck, pulled his face down to hers and kissed him gently before he went out into the deep snow. She watched him from the window as he bound his snowshoes to his feet, swiftly, efficiently, though his hands were already cold. He knew she was there, and following the old family custom, he turned to wave at her as he headed for the huge oak tree which marked the curve of the trail to the store. He sank to his knees at every step, and his snowshoes had to be lifted high for the next. Then, suddenly, he passed from her sight. She turned back to those in the room, weeping, and they knew their trial of waiting had begun.

All day they wondered why Theophile did not come. Jim was to stop at the store and tell him about going to town, so they had expected Vargatte to come to Big John as soon as he knew Jim had gone. But after supper he came. When he had removed his snowy wraps he told them frankly that Jim could not possibly get back until the morning. He was late in coming because he was planning to stay the night with Big John, and the three women were to go to bed and get some sleep. This they refused to do, but he persuaded Mrs. Big John to lie on a sofa in the corner, and finally coaxed the girls to go upstairs, promising he would waken them if there was the slightest indication that Big John felt weaker.

After a time the cabin became quiet, except for Big John's difficult breathing. Theophile saw that Mrs. Big John had fallen asleep and was relieved, for he knew she was almost ill from worry. At every sound he would sit up, alert and ready to open the door, but he heard only the whispering noise of the snow being hurled against the window by vagrant gusts of wind. The night was the longest he had ever known. Big John seemed to sleep, but Theophile was never sure. As he sat waiting for the late winter daylight to come through the windows he re-lived his friendship with Big John. He remembered the first day he and Delima had come to the Island. They were in the little, new store, trying to sort the boxes of goods which had preceded them. A poignant memory returned to him of his wife's sparkling beauty, her youth, and her first spasm of loneliness for the old home they had left. She was sitting on one of the big packing cases, smiling even as she wiped the tears from her eyes, and he was standing close to her, smiling too, when into the store stalked Big John with the mail-sack slung over his shoulder. He had given them one keen glance, had smiled and called, "Bo' jou'! I'm Big John, me, and this is the mail."

How courteously Delima had responded to his greeting. But Big John had seen the tears. Swiftly he had taken off his coat and offered to help them settle. Theophile could see him again as he had shoved and pulled, opened boxes, stacked groceries on shelves, all the while laughing and talking until they had called a halt for supper. From that night they had been friends, and that meaningful friendship had lasted through the years. Now Big John was dying, and soon he would be leaving the Island to join Delima. Theophile, as Jim had done earlier, thought many things as he sat by Big John's bedside.

When morning came, the women begged Theophile to stay with them until Jim returned with Father Lalliere, and he agreed. Big John woke soon after they had eaten breakfast, but refused the food they offered. Theophile could see that his strength was ebbing rapidly. Big John looked up at him and attempted to talk, but only a whisper came from his lips. Vargatte stooped low to hear. "See if they come. I grow weak," Big John requested, and though Theophile knew it was quite useless, he went to the door and looked long down the trail. The withered leaves on the bog oak rustled and a nuthatch called. No other sound broke the winter's stillness. He came back, shaking his head, and Big John again closed his eyes and seemed to sleep.

At noon, Big John asked Theophile to look again down the trail to see if Jim and the priest were coming. When Vargatte gently said they were not in sight, but might be just around the curve, Big John smiled. Well did he know his old friend Vargatte! "I cannot wait very long now, me," he whispered and Theophile knew that Big John spoke grim truth. If they did not come within a few hours they would indeed be too late to help Big John. That would be a bitter hurt for Father Lalliere.

Many, many times during that endless day Vargatte went out to see if the men were coming, and repeatedly he assured Big John that they must be very close and would soon arrive. Each reassurance made Big John smile faintly, again draw upon some deep, inner strength, and then reply, "They must come soon. I go before long, me." Theophile sat and prayed fervently that the priest would not be too late.

In the late afternoon the sun shot out from behind the clouds and sank in a sky of orange, yellow-blue and lavender. Soft rosy lights reflected on the brilliantly white birch trunks. Vargatte again looked from the open door, and there, plunging through the mountainous drifts came Jim, slowly and with terrible weariness breaking a trail for a slight, bent, tired figure which trudged valiantly behind him. A new and deeper reverence for his church surged up in Theophile's heart, and also for this gallant, black-robed, saintly man who represented that church, who had been their priest, their helper, their adviser and their friend for half a century. Father Lalliere could almost miraculously come to them through any sort of barrier when they needed him. Always their priest could find a way to reach them! Tears filled his eyes and ran over his cheeks as he returned to the living room and told Big John they were coming. They were turning under the big oak.

The early winter dusk followed the two struggling men into the cabin, which was lighted only by the firelight which flickered from the front of the open-stove. For weeks there had been no oil for the lamps. But Father Lalliere had been in their cabin many times; he would not stumble in the dusk. Jim stamped the snow noisily from his feet, and Celestina ran with the broom to brush away what clung to the shoes of the priest. Then, without a moment's rest they came forward. "Peace be to this house," said Father Lalliere.

The family and Theophile moved to another corner of the room. Father Lalliere took two blessed candles from his shabby bag and lighted them. As he placed the tapers upon the table, their light brought into the strong relief of a woodcut the faces of those gathered about in the small circle, and as they watched, they all saw a sudden halo appear around the noble head of this priest as he stood in front of the candles and searched again in his bag. Just as suddenly the halo faded, but the effect remained with them. Their reverence and solemnity could have been no more profound had they been in a cathedral. Here was a priest to lean upon; to trust to the uttermost. The significance of his presence made of their mean cabin a fitting place for a holy ceremony.

Father Lalliere found the oil for which he was searching. He went to the bed where Big John waited. For a time they talked with voices so low no one else could hear what was said. Then, at a motion of Father Lalliere's hand the others knelt.

"Sprinkle me, O Lord, with hyssop, ---"

Quietly, confidently, came Father Lalliere's voice through the gloom, so positively and reassuringly aware of the mercy of the great Father; his ministering hands were beautiful in the taper-light as he gave Big John the Last Sacrament.

"Look with favor, we beseech Thee, O Lord, upon Big John, Thy servant, failing from bodily weakness; and refresh the soul which Thou hast created, that being corrected by Thy chastisement, he may find himself cured by Thy healing. Through Christ ----"

"Chastisement!" That was what Jim had been trying to explain about Big John! The thought flashed also through Theophile's mind, but was forgotten as the prayers continued.

"Lord have mercy -----"
"Christ have mercy ----"
"Lord have mercy ----"

When the service was finished, the priest turned to include the others as his sonorous voice continued in prayer. And now, from the chair in which sat Jane Big John, came the low, weird moaning of the Indian lamentation of a bereaved woman. "Aih-ah------------aih-ah------------aih-ah" Ageless and eternal, it mingled with and became part of the sacred prayers. And as if Big John trusted his old friend the priest, and realized fully that he was safe and did not have to wait any longer, his breathing ceased without their knowing when. The candles flickered in the drafts which crept under the doors and the loose-fitting windows. The last prayer was finished. The lament went on. Big John had gone away, dropping his too-heavy burden at the End of the Trail of Life.

It was "Tomorrow," and Big John was dead.

CHAPTER XVII
AFTERGLOW

SYMBOL OF TIME PASSED

AFTERGLOW

Four Indian young people sat on the end of Big John's dock, all in the easy, graceful postures so typical of their race when they are at rest. Their figures were black against the flame of sunset, and their shadows became longer and darker across the dock-planks as the sun neared the rim of the earth. A new moon was slowly brightening as the theatrical mass of color which they were watching faded in the western sky. At something one of them said to another, they all turned toward the shore. There they saw the cold, familiar sights they had gazed upon from the day they were born. The small cabin squatted humpily in the clearing, and behind it the trail ---wider and more deeply worn than it used to be when Big John had built the house--- wound back until it curved and disappeared from their sight under the old oak, softly quiet now in its, new, red-velvet leaves. Tiny things they were, compared with the swifter-growing leaves of the huge maple in the front yard, the maple with the one branch which always turned red in the autumn before any other tree showed a sign of color. How many times had Young John asked "Why" about that maple tree!

On both sides of their clearing the shore-line was an unbroken stretch of green woods. Far down the lake loomed the Point, behind which Big John and Young John had found the Strange Woman when they had gone to find Old Red-Cow. In the direction of the Settlement, through the tree-tops they could see the white spire of the new church, just finished. In the evening light it seemed gilded. At last Father Lalliere's dream had become reality, and, even after he would have to give up his beloved work among them, they would always have an officiating priest who would come to them once each month. Blue-gray wood-smoke floated from the chimneys in the Settlement and from the Spring bonfires there. Kahnee stared at it as it wreathed dimly, mist-like through the air and over the hill. She turned to Jim. "Do you like the new store-keeper?" she asked. Jim nodded, without enthusiasm. "They are all right," he conceded, "but they are not Monsieur Theophile and Madame Delima Vargatte. They will never know us."

"What is the talk of the new Island ferry?" questioned Moses.

"It is now sure to come," said Jim thoughtfully, and the others could see that his thoughts were running as Big John's would have gone at the news. "In some ways it will be good. In other ways it will be bad. Many people will come to the Island, and many of them we will not want. Our quiet will vanish, and cars will run over the new-built roads. Trails will fade into nothingness. We Indians must hang tight to our land, no matter what changes come with the ferry."

"That is true," agreed Moses, and stared short-sightedly at Kahnee, desiring approbation for having expressed himself. She smiled at him, but absentmindedly.

Celestina's thoughts were closer home. "Do you think our mother is better and stronger?" she questioned all of them. She had fallen into their habits of speaking. Moses and Jim did not answer, and Kahnee shook her head. They sighed and turned again to the sunset. The garish color had faded into a soft rose which shaded into the purple-blue sky-line where the Canadian hills towered in the background. Then the sky suddenly became shot through with long beams of orange, as if a shuttered window on the horizon, somewhere behind those eternal hills, had opened a little and allowed a flood of celestial light to pour through. Celestina stared, enraptured. She reached out and caught Jim's arm. Her movement brought back to Kahnee's mind another scene on this same dock. She remembered Madeline reaching toward Telesphore as they had all sat watching another, similar sunset, and declaring that it was like a scene in a theater. Her throat ached with the longing to step back again into that moment. She clenched her big, awkward hands, and rose quickly to return to the house. But Celestina pointed toward the brilliant rays of orange light, beautiful beyond words. "That is where our father Big John is this very minute," she whispered reverently. "Can he see us here, do you think?"

Jim shrugged his shoulders. "So they say, those who are supposed to know best," he agreed. But the three Island Indians smiled, glanced at each other with secret knowledge in their eyes, and, turning unconsciously, looked far in the direction of Lake Superior, distant in the north, where float the Islands of the Indian dead. Jim turned again quickly to Celestina as if he felt guilty that she could never know or understand what was in their thoughts. "But I do not know," he continued gently. "Let us go now to the old mother. She does not like to be alone at the dusk-hour. She sees ---" he did not finish his thought.

  Slowly, but willingly, they all arose and walked up the short trail toward the tree-shadowed house, where the chair-fast old woman, Jane Big John, waited for them, rocking in her big rocker on the front stoop. The last tinge of color faded from the sky as they reached her. Kahnee loitered a moment behind the others. Back in the woods a white-throat fluted his evening call to the bright new moon.

EDITOR'S POSTSCRIPT

I would be remiss if I failed to mention to the reader of *Big John* that Florence McClinchey's first novel, *Joe Pete*, although widely acclaimed, was also met with a fair amount of controversy, especially from the American Indian community. And, to be honest, some of the same controversy surrounds the publication of *Big John*.

Joe Pete was published nearly 90 years ago; *Big John* was written over 70 years ago. During this period, and for centuries before, Native People suffered almost unimaginable deprivations across the entire Hemisphere – and it makes many people uncomfortable to read these two novels as Florence McClinchey exposes the cultural, psychic, and physical wounds of those deprivations.

But, contemporary criticism (and the criticism of *Joe Pete* during the first half of the 20th Century) should be tempered by an understanding of the dire situation faced by American Indians throughout the country --not only those living on Sugar Island-- in the early 20th Century.

The "Meriam Report," a 1928 Brookings Institute publication, revealed to a startled nation an American Indian experience of poverty, neglect, and hopelessness, due in large part to the monumental failure of government "Indian" policy from 1776 to this point in time.

The "Indian New Deal," instituted under the Roosevelt Administration, did alleviate the suffering of American Indians to some degree, but, as McClinchey revealed in both of her novels, the situation of many, if not most, of American Indians remained dire. In summary, this was the period during which the "Indians-as-a-Vanishing-Race" ideology was the dominant sentiment of even the most sympathetic observer.

So, yes, many readers are disturbed by the revelations of both *Joe Pete* and *Big John,* but, nevertheless, there are also many, including this Editor, who feel that it is better to confront the realities of the American Indian experience, both historic and contemporary, no matter how painful, than to suppress or ignore that grim reality.

Both of these masterful novels give the reader a glimpse of that depressing reality. It is for this reason that almost everyone who reviewed the manuscript --Native and non-Native, alike-- agreed that *Big John* should be published (and everyone also readily agreed that *Joe Pete* should be re-published; it is also now available from the Ziibi Press).

Phil Bellfy, PhD

Editor and Publisher of the Ziibi Press, Enrolled Member of the White Earth Band of Minnesota Chippewa, Co-Director of the Center for the Study of Indigenous Border Issues (CSIBI), and Professor Emeritus of American Indian Studies, Michigan State University.

ABOUT THE ZIIBI PRESS

The Ziibi Press is the publishing arm of CSIBI. "Ziibi" is the Ojibway word for "river," as in Mississippi (Ki-chi-ziibi; "a really big river").

CSIBI is focused on the political, economic, and cultural boundaries that separate Indigenous People from each other and the elements of the more dominant societies. Quite honestly, Sugar Island, situated on the US/Canada border is of utmost importance to our research and interest.

As the map in the beginning of this book shows, there are "Indian Reservations" on both sides of the border in this area. Indeed, many Native People of the region do not consider themselves to be "American" or "Canadian," but Anishnaabeg, the word we use to refer to ourselves, often translated as "The People Who Intend To Do Well."

Visit our website <ZiibiPress.com>
for information on our other publications.

This book was printed as a POD product
by Thomson-Shore, an employee-owned company,
head-quartered in Dexter, Michigan.
Visit them at <ThomsonShore.com>